W. J. Burley is a Cornishm
five generations. He start
went to Balliol to read zoo
leaving Oxford went into
retirement, was senior biology master in a large mixed
grammar school in Newquay. He created Inspector (now
Chief Superintendent) Wycliffe in 1966 and has featured
him in Cornish detective novels ever since. A major
television series featuring Superintendent Wycliffe was
recently shown on ITV.

Also by W. J. Burley

and published by Corgi Books

WYCLIFFE IN PAUL'S COURT

W. J. Burley

CORGI BOOKS

WYCLIFFE IN PAUL'S COURT
A CORGI BOOK   0   552   13433   3

Originally published in Great Britain by
Victor Gollancz Ltd.

PRINTING HISTORY
Victor Gollancz edition published 1980
Corgi edition published 1988
Corgi edition reprinted 1991
Corgi edition reprinted 1993
Corgi edition reprinted 1995

This book is set in Joanna 10/11pt by
Chippendale Type, Otley, West Yorkshire

Corgi Books are published by Transworld Publishers Ltd,
61–63 Uxbridge Road, Ealing, London W5 5SA,
in Australia by Transworld Publishers (Australia) Pty Ltd,
15–25 Helles Avenue, Moorebank, NSW 2170,
and in New Zealand by Transworld Publishers (NZ) Ltd,
3 William Pickering Drive, Albany, Auckland.

Printed and bound in Great Britain by
Cox & Wyman Ltd, Reading, Berkshire

CHAPTER ONE

Nobody in Falcon Street asked themselves where Willy Goppel had come from or how it was that the Dolls' House Shop had become as much a part of the street as St Olave's Church or the Old Mansion House or the market which closed the street to vehicles every Saturday. Willy Goppel had established himself as an institution, accepted uncritically. He spoke precise English with a German accent for, like the Bayreuth Festival, the Passion Play, Mad King Ludwig and the Nazi Party, Willy was Bavarian born. Many people in the street remembered his English wife but she had died years ago leaving him with a six-year-old son and some house property scattered about the city. His son Frederick, now a man, had left home though he still visited his father when he needed money. The property had grown too, both in value and extent, and though few people realized it, Willy was a wealthy man.

Willy lived over his shop in part of an old house of which the other, larger part, was occupied by the Wards who ran a sub post office and sold stationery, sweets and tobacco. A broad archway sliced through the ground floor of the house giving access to three modern dwellings built round a courtyard which had a splendid oak tree in the middle. A century before, the Paul family, carriers in a fair way of business, had lived in the house and kept their horses and waggons in appropriate buildings round the courtyard; now, the carrier business forgotten, those buildings had been replaced by three rather pleasant houses, secluded, not far from the city centre, and known as Paul's Court.

It had been another day of the September heatwave and in the cool of the evening Willy was out in his railed-off backyard, weeding and watering his sink gardens. He had started with one, now he had six, each laid out in an accepted style of landscape gardening with carefully chosen plants which, as far as possible, maintained the scale. On a patch of grass, protected by chicken-wire, Willy's guinea-pigs were getting their daily ration of the out-of-doors and at a little distance his marmalade cat sprawled in the sunshine, biting its paws.

The oak tree spread its green canopy over the middle of the courtyard and above a little red sports-car parked beneath it. The car belonged to Natalie Cole. Natalie lived with her fifteen-year-old daughter and Geoff Bishop in the house on the right-hand side of the Court. The other residents rather ostentatiously put their cars in the garages provided but such hints were lost on Natalie. Willy had only to raise his head from his sink gardens to see her through the wide open window of her living-room. She was seated at the table eating something, almost certainly something out of a tin, for Natalie was not a devoted housekeeper. She had spent the afternoon sunbathing on her verandah and, as on other days during this week of unusually hot weather, she had started by wearing a bikini and finished naked on the folding bed.

Marty Fiske came ambling across the Court and leaned on the fence, watching Willy at work, his eyes unwavering and vacant. Everybody treated Marty as a child though he was eighteen and powerfully built.

'You give the flowers water, Mr Goppy?'

'Yes, Marty.'

Marty laughed, gobbling his words, 'Flowers like to drink, don't they, Mr Goppy?'

'They must have water, Marty.'

The same conversation, with minor variations, took place every time Marty happened to come along when Willy was tending his plants.

Mrs Fiske's voice came from the far end of the Court: 'Marty! Where are you? Your meal is on the table ... Marty!'

She could not see them because of the tree.

'I got to go now, that was mother.'

'Good night, Marty.'

'Good night, Mr Goppy.'

Willy's part of the house comprised his shop, his workshop and a little hall on the ground floor; living-room, kitchen and bathroom on the first floor, and two bedrooms on the second. There was a square stairwell and a rather impressive staircase, relic of the original house. He went upstairs to the kitchen, washed his hands and started to prepare the evening meal – lamb chop, boiled potatoes, greens and mint sauce. His tastes in food had been wholly anglicized. The cat, too well fed to be importunate, curled up under the table.

Willy was below average height, thin, with sparse grey hair, dark eyes and sallow skin. His features were rather large for his face giving him a solemn yet clownish appearance. His kitchen was separated by only a thin partition from the Wards' and their son, Henry, was in his bedroom playing jazz records very loud. Willy whistled through his teeth in time to the beat – not that he had a taste for jazz but he liked to be reminded of the life next door. He had watched the Ward children – Henry and Alison – growing up and he was fond of them both; they called him 'Uncle'.

In the Ward's living-room Alison was laying the table for their evening meal. Her mother had just come up from the shop and was in the kitchen preparing to serve the meal she had put in the oven earlier. Alison was sixteen and still at school; she wore the regulation school summer uniform – a short-sleeved frock in a small brown-and-white check; she had straight fair hair which draped itself over her shoulders, a peaches-and-cream complexion and serious blue eyes.

'How were things at school today?' Her mother's voice came from the kitchen.

'All right, I suppose. We had a history test on our holiday work and I didn't like it much.'

'I thought history was your best subject.'

Alison paused long enough to prevent the irritation she felt being apparent in her voice. 'It was all on the seventeenth century, nothing on the eighteenth I spent so much time on.'

'Never mind dear, I expect you did as well as the others.'

Julia Ward was a well meaning woman who never tired of looking on the bright side. At nineteen she had won a beauty contest and when the interviewer asked her what she wanted most in life she had answered: 'I just want to make people happy.'

There were four places at the table; Alison's father would come up from the shop at the last minute, probably when the soup was already on the table. Her brother Henry, who was seventeen, was up in his room listening to old records of Duke Ellington, his latest craze.

Four table knives, four forks, four soup spoons, four side-plates with green and gilt edging and four table napkins ... Abruptly she experienced one of those moments when she seemed to exist outside herself, able to see herself as a stranger. She saw that girl who went to school and worked hard to learn things she did not want to know, the girl who spent two hours every night doing homework, the girl who helped her mother with household chores, the girl who next year would be in the sixth form working for 'A' levels . . . 'It's your future you've got to think of, dear.' What future? *Whose* future? What would it be like to be the real Alison Ward? What would she do?

It was the time of day when the living-room caught the sun and golden light flooded in, seeming to vibrate to the brash rhythms of the music upstairs.

'Alison! What are you thinking of, love? Your father will be up at any minute and the table not laid . . .'

'Sorry.'

Natalie Cole was taking a shower; when she had finished she dried herself and walked through into the bedroom to look at her body in a full-length mirror. There was nothing narcissistic about the minute scrutiny to which she subjected herself; her body was one of her assets and, in the nature of things, a wasting one. Though not seriously so – yet.

At thirty-two she still looked girlish, her waist measurement had stayed at twenty-two ever since she had been interested enough to remember, and she had the lithe figure of a dancer; her belly was flat, her navel perfect and the pubic hair-line was low with no tendency to creep upward. A tiny appendix scar marred her right side. She remembered that surgeon: 'You'll have to wear a bit more bikini, young lady.' Smug, leering bastard! Her breasts were firm and full . . .

Her skin was changing though, losing that velvet elasticity, especially on her legs and neck. She studied her face; she was no longer a pretty girl but was she a beautiful woman? Her jet black hair, just short of shoulder length, seemed to cling and mould itself to her head, framing her face in a classical oval. She had dark eyes which mirrored every subtle change in the light and her skin had a warm colour, as though lightly tanned, neither swarthy nor pale . . . So far so good; but

9

there was something – something about the set of her mouth which was becoming more pronounced . . . If she had seen it in another woman she would have said, 'There goes a bitch!'

'Christ! I'm getting morbid.'

She turned to pick up her wrap from the bed and saw her daughter standing in the doorway watching her. Yvette was fifteen, slim and dark like her mother but seventeen years younger. The expression Natalie had surprised on her daughter's face annoyed her; a look of detached appraisal.

'What do you want?'

'To tell you I'm going out.'

'Have you done your homework?' The question was part of a prescribed ritual, not intended to be answered.

'Who are you going with?'

'A girl.'

'Not the Ward boy?'

'No.'

'You haven't had a meal.'

'I'll get something out.'

Natalie watched her go. Jeans and a T-shirt; no bra, of course; and across the front of the T-shirt: 'Restricted Area', stencilled in red.

'Poor little bastard!' Natalie's sympathy was not so much for her daughter as for her sex. She called out, 'Don't be late, Yvette!'

The front door slammed.

A few minutes later a car drove into the Court and she went to the window to see who it was. A Rover 2600, maroon and spotless. Martin Fiske, Marty's father, was a business consultant with a firm of his own. The Fiskes lived in the house which faced up the Court. Natalie watched him put his car away and saw him come out of the garage, carrying his briefcase. Fiske was in his early forties, an ex-rugby player going slightly to seed; thinning hair, a self-important manner and the beginnings of a paunch. He wore a dove-grey light-weight suit, silk shirt and tie and suede shoes.

'Smooth bastard!'

Fiske came downstairs from washing his hands and entered the dining-room just as his wife was bringing two bowls of soup from the kitchen. The table was laid for two.

'Where's Marty?'

'In his room; I gave him his meal early because I know how much you dislike having to eat with him.'

Joan Fiske, at forty-eight, was thin, angular and careworn. Her manner towards her husband was a curious blend of subservience and aggression, like a dog who is sporadically ill-treated.

Fiske sat down, tucked in his napkin and tasted the soup before adding pepper and salt.

'I want to talk to you, Martin.'

'You surprise me. What about?'

She was crumbling a bread-roll into tiny fragments. 'It's about that woman, she's been sunbathing on her verandah again, in the nude.'

Fiske soaked a piece of bread in his soup and chewed it.

'It's Marty I worry about. I mean, that sort of stimulation could lead to anything.'

'I don't suppose he even notices the woman.'

Mrs Fiske became irritated. 'Of course he notices! He came in this afternoon and said "That lady out there with no clothes." You know what the psychologist told us as well as I do.'

Fiske finished his soup and dabbed his lips with his napkin. His wife went on: 'What a way for the mother of a young girl to carry on! But what can you expect from a woman who earns her living in a nightclub?'

'She happens to own the club.'

'What difference does that make? Those places are no better than brothels.'

Fiske turned his cold, fishy eyes on his wife. 'Of course, you know about these things.'

Mrs Fiske shifted her ground. 'I can't imagine why you brought her here in the first place.'

Fiske cleared his throat but did not raise his voice. 'I did not bring her here; I met her in the course of business; she happened to say that she was looking for a house and I mentioned that there was one vacant in the Court.'

Joan Fiske pushed away her soup scarcely touched, collected her husband's plate and went through to the kitchen. There was no conversation while she served the second course, veal cutlets with beans and sauté potatoes, but when they were seated once more she took up where she had left off. 'That man who lives with her, what does he do?'

Fiske sighed. 'Bishop? I must have told you a dozen times, he runs a garage in Fenton Street; he sells second-hand cars and hires out cars and vans.'

'He's hardly ever home. I never see him.'

Fiske helped himself to more potatoes and gravy; his wife picked at her food then put down her knife and fork with an air of finality. 'Anyway, I went to see Mrs Ward at the post office this afternoon. I told her about the sunbathing and I asked her to back me up in a protest.'

'You did *what?*' Fiske stopped eating to glare at his wife in sudden anger. 'How many times have I told you not to get involved in gossip and squabbles in the Court? I can't afford it! These people are clients of mine. I handle all Natalie Cole's business as well as Bishop's; and Willy Goppel is one of my best accounts. They're my clients and your bread-and-butter. Do you understand?'

12

Mrs Fiske went over to the defensive. 'I'm sure I've never done anything to upset Willy Goppel.'

'No, but you will. You'll think of something. His cat will shit on our grass or dig up a dandelion in your bloody flower-bed.'

Joan Fiske stared down at her plate and her features crumpled on the verge of weeping.

'For God's sake don't start howling! I've had enough to put up with for one day.'

From upstairs came a low moaning sound; Marty was singing to himself as he made one of his simple jigsaws for the thousandth time.

The house on the fourth side of the Court was occupied by an elderly couple, the Hedleys. They were tall, lean and desiccated. Until four of five years back a nephew of Mrs Hedley, orphaned at the age of ten, had lived with them and they had brought him up. Now he and Willy Goppel's son, Frederick, shared a flat in another part of the city. Mr Hedley was a retired council official while his wife came of a family with pretensions in the world of the arts and music and was considered to have married beneath her. As if to make the point their radio played classical music through much of the day when Mrs Hedley was not giving *bravura* piano performances of her favourite composers. The music furnished a subdued background to the other life of the Court. The Hedleys had their main meal at mid-day and he seemed to spend a lot of time moving uneasily about the house like a caged cat. From time to time he appeared on his verandah where he would stand, staring into space for ten minutes or more, a cigarette dangling from his lower lip.

The post office Wards had reached the dessert stage of their meal.

13

'Mrs Fiske was in this afternoon, while you were at the bank.'

Edward Ward was eating strawberry mousse with a preoccupied air and his wife had to repeat her remark.

'What did she want?'

'She bought a few stamps but she wanted us to join her in a complaint about Mrs Cole.'

'Because she keeps her car under the tree? Seems a bit childish, doesn't it?'

'It wasn't about the car; she objects to Mrs Cole sunbathing in the nude on her verandah. She's afraid it will upset Marty.'

'I shouldn't think Marty would notice one way or the other. Anyway, what did you say to her?'

'I said that being in business we couldn't afford to get involved with disagreements.'

Ward nodded. 'Quite right too.'

'Does she sunbathe in the nude?' Alison looked across at her mother.

'Apparently. I haven't seen her.'

'Have you seen her, Henry?' Alison turned to her brother.

Henry, with sandy hair and freckles, blushed easily and he did so now to his intense annoyance. 'No.'

'You seemed to be getting on well with her the other morning.'

'I helped her to start her car, that was all. She had a dodgy contact in the distributor.'

'Was that what it was? She seemed very grateful, I was watching: she positively drooled. Yvette will be jealous.'

Henry was angry. 'Why must you always—?'

Mrs Ward laughed. 'Don't take any notice of her, Henry; you ought to know her by now.'

Henry got up from his chair. 'I'm sick of her getting at me all the time. What business is it of hers anyway?' He strode out of the room, slamming the door behind him.

Alison was contrite.

'You really do tease the poor boy, Alison.'

'I'm sorry, but he always rises to it, it's like putting your money in a slot machine. I'll go and say I'm sorry when he's had a chance to cool off.'

The sound of another Duke Ellington record came from upstairs.

Mrs Ward looked at her daughter. 'Is he still seeing that Yvette?'

'Every day; we all three go to the same school.'

'Don't be clever, dear; you know exactly what I mean.'

'Yes, mother, and I'm not going to spy on him and report back.'

Mrs Ward was hurt. 'As if I would want you to! It's just that I don't like the idea of him getting mixed up with those people. I've no doubt the little girl is very nice but her mother . . .'

'I don't think he goes out with her mother.'

'Alison! You really are very rude.'

Henry lay on his bed listening to the Duke Ellington version of Grieg's Peer Gynt.

'What's the matter? Can't you get it to start?'

He had been on his way to school and she was trying to start her little red car.

'I don't know what's the matter with it and Geoff has gone to work. Geoff Bishop was the man who lived with her.

'Shall I have a look?'

'Do you understand these things?'

'I'm doing a course on car maintenance at school.'

'Really?'

She was wearing a trouser suit in some silky material the colour of flame.

After a few minutes with his head under the bonnet he emerged and said, 'Now try.'

The engine started first kick. 'My! You must have oily

fingers or whatever it takes!' She looked up at him from the driving seat of her little car. 'You must come over sometime for a drink.'

He stood by the car door, red faced. 'I'd like that.'

She saw that he meant it and was amused. 'You've been going out with Yvette, haven't you?'

'Once or twice.'

She smiled. 'Well, come over on Sunday afternoon after you've had lunch.'

'Thanks.'

'Can I give you a lift?'

'No, thanks, I've got my moped.'

The Duke Ellington record ran out and in the ensuing silence he could hear the subdued whine of the little lathe Willy Goppel used for making his dolls' house fittings. There was a tap at the door and his sister came in. She stood by the bed, looking down at him. 'Sorry, Harry-boy.'

He picked at a loose thread in his jeans. 'It doesn't matter.'

'I was only teasing.'

'I know.'

She turned to go.

'Ali, she asked me to come over for a drink on Sunday afternoon.'

'Are you going?'

'Would you?'

'Why not? Are you afraid she'll seduce you or something? In any case, Yvette will be there, won't she?'

He did not answer at once then he said, 'I know it sounds daft but I had the impression it wasn't going to be like that.'

'You mean she really does fancy you?'

'Now you're at it again!'

'No, I'm not; from what I've heard about her you could be right.'

He swung his legs off the bed. 'Hell! I thought life got simpler as you got older.'

His sister grinned down at him. 'Never mind, boy, when rape is inevitable, just lie back and enjoy it.'

He chuckled despite himself. 'Where did you get that one?'

'Confucius, he say.'

'I don't believe it.'

They were silent for a moment or two while they both listened to the whirring of Willy Goppel's lathe.

Alison said, 'I'd better do some homework.'

'You make me feel lazy.'

'I've got 'O' levels in November.'

'You'll be all right, Ali; when they dished out the brains to this family you got a double ration.'

'Idiot!'

Alison's room was on the same floor. It was large and she had decorated it to her own taste. The floorboards were varnished with three or four rugs scattered about; there was an armchair with a blue-linen loose cover to match the bedspread; varnished shelves held her school books and a large number of paperbacks, and she had a table and chair by the window. A magnificent three-storied dolls' house occupied one corner of the room, a masterpiece of a dolls' house furnished exquisitely in late Victorian or Edwardian style on a scale of one-twelfth. The dolls' house had been a tenth birthday present from Uncle Willy and six years later she was still under its spell. She could lose count of time sitting on the floor, peering into the rooms and imagining the lives of the people who lived in them; people for whom time had stood still on some summer afternoon when there were still nannies and children had nurseries where there was always a giant rocking-horse and mother had leg-of-mutton sleeves to her dress and father wore tight trousers and side-whiskers.

She sprawled on a rug with her biology textbook.

'In the duodenum the food is mixed with secretions from the walls of the duodenum itself and from the pancreas. . . .'

She closed the book on her finger and recited the enzymes and what they did, moving her lips soundlessly.

It was all very well talking about sex equality but women still had to have babies. In a confused and inarticulate way she felt that women like Natalie Cole somehow registered a protest and she was both repelled and intrigued.

Willy Goppel switched off his lathe and gathered up the sixty or seventy little pieces of wood he had turned; they were balusters for the staircase of a commissioned dolls' house. He moved from his bench by the window to a large table which occupied most of the workshop where the house was under construction. The staircase rose in a graceful double curve from the hall to a gallery which went most of the way round the first floor. Willy started to insert the balusters into little holes already drilled to receive them; the newel posts were in place and now came the moment of truth when he would fit the handrails.

Scufflings and scratchings, whistles, little grunts and cries came from the animal cages against one wall of the workshop. In addition to his guinea-pigs Willy kept hamsters and gerbils and, in heated vivaria, geckos, skinks and a variety of small snakes. Outside the light was fading but in the workshop there were two power-ful lamps with green shades. Usually when he was working Willy felt completely relaxed, totally absorbed and regardless of any other care, but tonight a nagging concern troubled him so that he could not concentrate. His hand trembled and one of the balusters slipped from his fingers.

18

'Verflucht!'

It was rare for him to swear at all, rarer still for him to swear in German. Nowadays he seemed to think mostly in English.

That morning, before opening the shop, he had set out as usual to buy the things he needed for the day. He had never gone in for bulk purchases nor troubled himself with refrigerators or freezers so he lived from hand to mouth. He preferred it that way; he enjoyed his morning stroll, visiting the neighbourhood shops, stopping for a yarn here and there and picking up the news of the street. As he was passing under the archway he had heard Natalie Cole's car behind him; she drew level and stopped, waiting for her chance to filter into the traffic along Falcon Street. She was beside him, looking up with an amused, faintly sardonic smile on her face.

'Guten Morgen Herr Hauptmann.'

Her pronunciation was execrable but her meaning was clear and he was so taken aback that he remained standing foolishly long after she had joined the stream of traffic. He tried to tell himself that it was a joke. After all, Englishmen sometimes addressed each other as 'Skipper' or even 'Cap'n' without meaning anything by it, but the words laboriously repeated in German . . . It was too much of a coincidence.

A month ago a thief had stolen from his workshop desk a cigar box containing eighty pounds in cash and souvenirs of his youth in Germany. He had not reported the theft to the police.

Willy picked up one of the two stair rails he had carved, a thin snake of wood worked to the right section and curved in two planes with little holes drilled to fit over the tops of the balusters. A few moments of intense concentration and it was securely in place. He reached for the second rail.

Over the years, without actually saying so, he had

19

allowed people to believe that he was a German Jew, a victim of the *Totenkopfverbande*. Many times he had been asked, 'What was it really like in the camps?' And he had always answered, 'I managed to avoid that, thank God!' But if that was not a lying answer it was certainly an evasion of the truth. Now, after more than thirty years!

He looked at the second rail in his hand as though it was something strange and unfamiliar then pulled himself together and set about fitting it to the staircase.

The street-door bell rang and he went through to the shop to answer it but he did not switch on the shop light. He opened the door and his son, Frederick, followed him in.

'I saw the light from the street so I thought I'd look in and see how you are.'

Willy led the way through to the workshop. Frederick was in his twenties, slim and small and fair – rather effeminate. He stood by the dolls' house, looking at it without interest.

'What brings you here, boy?'

'I told you, I just happened to be passing.'

Willy said nothing for a while, not until he had completed the fitting of the second handrail, then he turned to his son. 'Did you happen to be passing about a month ago?'

'I don't know what you mean, it's longer than that since I was here.'

Willy looked him straight in the eyes. 'Somebody came in here while I was out doing my shopping and stole eighty pounds in money, some papers and a few souvenirs from my desk.' He nodded towards an old-fashioned high desk with a flap-lid which stood against the wall.

The young man looked scared.

'You don't think it was me? Why should I steal from you? It could have been anybody. You go out and leave the shop door unlocked. Anybody can walk in and help themselves.'

Willy nodded. 'Somebody did. I wonder how they knew where to look.'

Freddie recovered a little of his poise. 'It's obvious, dad. Anybody after valuables would look in a desk, wouldn't they?'

'The desk was locked, somebody forced the lock with a chisel.'

Willy held his son's gaze for a little longer. 'You don't have to steal from me, Frederick.'

'But I swear—'

Willy sighed. 'No need to swear, Frederick. In any case it's not so much the money as the papers I'm concerned about.'

'You should lock the shop when you go out, dad.'

'I do – now. When I remember.'

There was an interval of silence then Freddie said, 'What did the police say?'

'They did not say anything because I did not tell them.'

Willy spent a little time lightly polishing the handrail he had just fitted before turning to his son again. 'Are you in some sort of trouble?'

'No trouble – no.'

'Short of money?'

Frederick laughed uneasily. 'Who isn't?'

Willy took out his wallet and drew from it three five-pound notes. 'Will that see you through?'

'It will help; thanks, dad.'

Willy sighed. 'I only help you, boy, to keep you out of trouble. You understand?'

'Yes, dad; thanks.'

'In a few minutes I shall be going upstairs to prepare my supper; there is enough for two if you care to join me.'

'No, dad, I can't; I've got to meet somebody.'

Much later, after Willy and the other inhabitants of the Court were in bed, the little red sports-car erupted through the archway and screeched to a halt beneath the tree. There was an interval before Natalie Cole got out, swaying with tiredness.

CHAPTER TWO

Yvette came downstairs, her mother and Geoff Bishop were still in bed. She went to the kitchen, took a bottle of milk from the refrigerator and emptied half of it into a glass.

Saturday morning; no school for two whole days. All week she had looked forward to being free of the boredom of school, now the day stretched ahead – blank; at least until evening. She found a sponge cake in a tin, cut off a slice and took it with her milk to the verandah. It was another fine day. Marty Fiske was playing with Willy Goppel's cat, trying to get it to chase a piece of string, but though the cat watched, green eyed, it would not budge.

The sun, the tree, the cobbles, the grass, the houses and the blue sky had a quality of unchanging stillness; she seemed to be enveloped, smothered by a *now* which threatened to go on for evermore.

'Nothing will ever happen, nothing will ever change.'

' 'lo, 'vette.' Marty grinned foolishly; he was always embarrassed when he spoke to her.

It was absurd, a man performing the antics and adopting the postures of a shy little boy. She made no allowances and she was brusque, 'Hullo.'

'I'm playing with Mr Goppy's cat.'

'So I see.'

'I like cats.'

The window of the Wards' living-room over the archway was wide open; she could hear a radio or record player and from time to time she saw Alison pass the window. The Ward family had had their breakfasts, all four of them sitting round a table together. Now Mr and Mrs Ward were in the shop and Alison was clearing away. Later she would wash up. Afterwards she would spend two or three hours on her school work, then lunch. In the afternoon she would meet a couple of other girls from school and they would go off cycling together. In the evening they might go mad and visit a coffee bar.

'God!'

All the same, the Wards were a family, they held together and counted on each other. When she was with Henry it was 'We' do this or 'We' do the other. She both resented and envied his calm assumption of belonging.

She finished her cake and drank her milk. 'If only there was something I really *wanted*!'

She left her empty glass on the verandah and went down the steps, across the Court and let herself into Willy Goppel's yard. His back door was open and she drifted into his workshop.

'Good morning, Yvette. You are early this morning. I have not started to clean out the cages.'

'I'll do it.'

'But I cannot let you do it all, child—'

She snapped, 'I'll do it! And I wish you wouldn't call me "child".'

Willy was not in the least put out. 'All right, Yvette, thank you. You are a great help to me with the animals. You have a way with them which is rare. It is only that people should not have pets unless they are prepared to look after them themselves. I think.'

'There are lots of things people shouldn't do.'

Yvette liked Willy, partly because he was a loner like herself, partly because he did not ask questions or offer advice. But she was frequently rude to him because she was afraid that unless she kept her distance she might drop her guard and talk to him – really talk.

Willy hovered while she started on the guinea-pigs who were whistling to be fed.

'Why don't you get off to the market?'

'All right, if you are quite sure . . .'

'I'm sure.'

Willy was back in a few minutes wearing cavalry-twill trousers and a linen jacket. He stood for a moment watching the lithe figure of the girl as she went about her task. As she stooped, jeans and T-shirt parted company disclosing an area of slim bare back. She seemed so vulnerable that Willy was moved to say, 'Take care of yourself, Yvette.'

'Don't worry, I always do.'

For once the market had a fine day; there were stalls on both sides from one end of Falcon Street to the other. Through traffic was banned and residents' cars had to take their chance, nudging their way along. Willy closed his shop on Saturdays and in the morning he liked to wander through the street chatting with the stallholders. They were a close-knit community and in some cases the pitches had been handed down from father to son through three or even four generations.

' 'Morning, Willy! I'm busy now but if you look in on your way back I'll keep some nice toms for you. Full of green juice – just as you like 'em.'

There was little chance to talk to the men on the fruit and vegetable stalls who were kept busy by house-wives, but the others – selling books, records, fancy goods, clothes and second-hand junk of every description – were glad to chat. It took him nearly an hour to work his way a hundred yards along the street and it was mid-day before he reached his favourite stall. It belonged to a tall, scholarly-looking man who wore a black Homburg hat and was universally known as the

Professor. His stock-in-trade was well above the average and included stamps, coins, medals and a range of books some of which justified the tattered notice, 'Of Antiquarian Interest'.

While the usual, rather elaborate civilities were being exchanged, Willy looked over the display. His eye was caught by a string of German war medals and the Professor must have noticed the sudden change in his expression.

'Are you interested? I bought them only last week. He spoke in a cultured voice, enunciating each syllable distinctly.

'They are mine,' Willy said.

'Yours? You mean you sold them?'

'No, they were stolen from a desk in my workshop.'

The Professor's grey eyes widened. 'My dear fellow! I had no idea that you . . . You must allow me to make immediate restitution. I insist!' He held out the medals in a grandiloquent gesture but Willy did not take them.

'No, I do not want them back. You are welcome to them.'

'But I cannot possibly allow such a thing! They are yours, my friend.'

A gentlemanly argument ensued but Willy was adamant. 'They revive memories best forgotten. I was foolish to keep them and I do not want them back.'

'If you really mean that . . . '

'I do,' Willy said, 'I do.'

The Professor looked from the medals to Willy and back again. He was embarrassed because he had always looked upon Willy as a victim of the Nazis. 'I had no idea . . . You must have had a very distinguished war record, my friend, they did not hand out these for guard duties.'

Willy was terse. 'You do not have to earn medals to own them. You should know that; such things are bought and sold.'

The Professor adjusted his Homburg. 'Of course! How foolish of me! There was I beginning to think that at some time you and I might have tried to kill each other.'

'That,' said Willy, 'is very unlikely.' He turned his back on the medals. 'Now, I wish that you will do me a favour.'

'Anything.'

'I was interested in the medals because they were taken at the same time as some papers which I value, also a photograph. Could it be that you have these also?'

The Professor shook his head. 'I am afraid not, Willy. Only the medals came my way.'

'You know who sold them to you?'

'Unfortunately not. I had never seen him before; he came into my shop and I bought the medals over the counter for cash.' There was a pause before the Professor enquired, 'How far are the police involved?'

'They are not. I did not report the theft.'

The other looked surprised. 'That is good, it makes it easier for me to help you. Tell me what it is you wish.'

'To recover my papers, or at least, to find out what has happened to them.'

The Professor nodded. 'That is reasonable. I will see what can be done. And thank you, my friend, for not making trouble.'

'Trouble,' said Willy, 'I wish to avoid.'

Freddie Goppel and Toby 'Pongo' Lennon lived on the third floor of a near-derelict house in Telfer Street, behind the pannier market. The window of their living-room looked over the narrow street, across the roofs of the market, to an office block a couple of hundred yards away. The room was shabby and dirty, furnished out of junk shops and rarely ventilated or cleaned. Toby, who had lived there since leaving his aunt's house in Paul's

Court, was in his late twenties; he had the build of a gorilla, a thatch of coarse, black hair, a bushy beard and moustache through which his lips protruded pink and moist.

Freddie was looking out of the window at the view which even the sunshine could not redeem. 'I went to see my old man last night.'

Pongo said nothing.

'He was nattering on about his papers. What were those papers, Pongo?'

'Don't you know?'

'You know damn well I can't read German.'

Lennon laughed. 'The boy is called Frederick Goppel but he can't read German.'

'The old man was against it. He wanted me, as he put it, "to up grow into a proper little Englishman".'

'And instead you grew up into a proper little rat. You must be a sore disappointment to him, Freddie.'

'But you can read German. What are they, Pongo?'

'Something to keep us warm next winter, perhaps?'

Freddie looked scared. 'You don't mean blackmail, Pongo? What's he done? I mean, it's one thing to help ourselves to a few quid now and then but . . . '

Lennon stood up and lumbered across the room. He took Freddie's head between his huge hands and looked into his eyes. 'You want to live easy, Freddie, without soiling your dainty hands.' He spoke quietly and without heat. 'Sometimes I wonder why I don't smash that pale, appealing mug of yours once and for all. What would you say to that, pretty boy?'

Freddie's face was surprisingly untroubled. 'Kiss me, Hardy.'

Lennon roared with laughter. 'You win, Freddie, boy! I was only kidding about your old man anyway. But leave the thinking to me – okay?'

'Okay, Pongo.'

Lennon returned to his chair. Freddie's eyes followed him. 'I wish I knew what goes on in that great head of yours, Pongo.'

Lennon laughed. 'Don't worry about it, boy. Pongo will look after you.' He glanced at his watch. 'It's half-twelve, what about going along to the boozer for a pint and a snack?'

*   *   *

On Sunday afternoon rain fell in a continuous drizzle from leaden clouds which scarcely cleared the top of St Olave's steeple. An hour after lunch Henry crossed the Court and went up the steps to Natalie's door. It stood very slightly open. He knocked and felt that he was being watched from every direction though he knew that his parents were in the front of the house and that Alison had gone out. The Fiskes could not see him and Uncle Willy would be taking his afternoon nap. That left the Hedleys, the zombie like old couple, and Mr Hedley was there on his verandah, staring into space, standing first on one foot, then on the other.

There was no answer to his knock so he pushed the door wider and stepped inside. He felt like a nervous, amateur burglar.

'It's me, Henry Ward.'

'I'm in the living-room.'

He went through the door to his right into a room which was almost wholly white. Only the pictures on the walls offered relief in different shades of blue and green. She was seated in one of the white upholstered armchairs in front of a massive, bright steel, coal-effect electric fire. She wore an acid-green sleeveless frock and she looked at him over the rim of a glass which contained ice cubes and, presumably, whisky. There was a drinks table by her chair.

29

He stood, gauche and tongue-tied.

'So you've come.'

'You said that I might.'

'What will you drink – whisky?'

'I'd rather have a beer if I may.'

She pointed to a white cabinet. 'Help yourself.'

In this cabinet, apart from a great variety of drinks and glasses, there was a miniature refrigerator stocked with beer and minerals. He opened a can and filled a glass then went to stand near her. Her eyes were puffy and her mouth seemed slack. When she spoke she did so carefully as though it involved some slight difficulty.

'You needn't look at me like that; I'm all right, it's just that I've had too much to drink.'

'Why?'

The question seemed to surprise her. 'Do I have to have a reason for drinking too much?'

He was embarrassed. 'I'm sorry, I suppose not.'

'But I do have one – the best; I'm bored – B O R E D ! Are you ever bored, Henry?'

'Sometimes.'

She looked at her glass which was empty and returned it to the table. 'Do you have to stand there like a bloody statue? Don't you bend in the middle or something?'

'Sorry.'

He sat down and she went on: 'If you are expecting to see Yvette she's not here; she's gone off somewhere for the afternoon and Geoff is at the garage so we've got the place to ourselves. Cosy, isn't it?'

'Very nice.'

She chuckled. 'I like you, Henry. You don't have a regular girl-friend?'

'Not a regular one – no.'

'Lucky devil! Just shopping around.'

'No, it's not like that either.'

'Isn't it, Henry?' She was watching him with her large

dark eyes which were partly veiled by their lids. 'Why did you come this afternoon?'

'Because you said—'

'Never mind what I said; why did you come?'

'I suppose it was because I think you are a very attractive . . .' he hesitated over the choice of a word then said, 'girl.'

She laughed. 'Thank you, Henry. You'll have to watch it, you have a way with you.'

He felt himself flushing and cursed inwardly. He finished his beer. 'I suppose I'd better be getting back.'

'Why?'

'I don't know really.'

She got up and came over to his chair to stand by him, ruffling his hair. 'You're a nice boy, Henry. I'm going upstairs to lie down and you can come up in ten minutes if you want to.' She paused at the door. 'First on the left at the top of the stairs. Suit yourself.'

He sat there trying to make up his mind what to do; more accurately, trying to muster the courage not to cut and run. It was one thing to get involved with a girl at a party; quite another to go upstairs with a married woman. Without having made a conscious decision he found himself climbing the stairs. He hesitated at the door which was partly open, hoping that she would speak, but no sound came from the bedroom. He went in and stood just inside the door. In the grey afternoon light, filtered by a slatted blind, he could not see clearly at first. The furniture, the blinds, the carpet and the bedclothes were all white; she seemed to have a passion for white; but the room was untidy, littered with clothes, and there was an indefinable smell over and above that of make-up and toiletries; elusive, intimate.

She was in bed and he could see only her black hair on the pillow. He went over to the bed. She was holding the bedclothes round her shoulders, looking up at him, unsmiling, her eyes solemn and questioning. He did not know what to do then, with a sudden movement, she uncovered her breasts; her body appeared dusky white, slim and infinitely supple.

'Aren't you going to undress?'

He had never before been with anyone experienced in the art of love and Natalie was a revelation. He surrendered himself in luxurious abandonment to a rising tide of sexuality, he was carried along by it, engulfed, then swept into a limbo of consciousness where there was nothing left but the rhythm of his pounding heart.

When it was over quietness possessed him like a narcotic drug, seeping through his tissues, neutralizing, quelling, calming, until he began to feel deliciously relaxed. He saw the room through half-closed lids, filled with pearly grey shadows, insubstantial, ethereal. He seemed to float in a cloudy, opalescent world: soft and sensual but not cloying and wished that it would go on for ever.

'Thank you.'

'For what?'

'For everything.'

She ruffled his hair. 'Silly boy!'

Then, suddenly, Natalie was asleep, her breasts pressed against him, his sex against her thigh; the weight of her body lay across one of his legs. Afraid to move, he became rigid. Where they touched their bodies were moist and clammy. Natalie slept with her lips parted and she breathed with a slight, tremulous snore. He could smell the whisky on her breath. Abruptly his euphoria vanished and disenchantment chased away romance. He began to feel ashamed.

With infinite caution he edged out of bed, collected his clothes and went to the bathroom where he sponged himself down and dressed. Then, with his shoes in his hand, like a character in a bedroom farce, he crept out. When he was half-way down the stairs the front door opened and Yvette stood in the hall looking up at him. The situation was as hackneyed as a mother-in-law joke but none the less painful for that. Her understanding was immediate and complete.

'Don't mind me, I live here.'

That evening Geoff Bishop crossed the Court in the rain to call on Willy Goppel. Although Bishop had lived with Natalie for upwards of two years he had never exchanged half-a-dozen words with Willy.

'Mr Bishop, isn't it?'

Bishop was uncharacteristically anxious to do the right thing. 'I came to the back door, seeing it's Sunday and the shop is shut . . . '

'Back door or front, they both lead to the same place,' Willy said. 'You want to see me, Mr Bishop?'

'About my garage.'

'Ah! You'd better come in.'

Bishop followed him through the workshop, looking curiously at the dolls' house under construction. 'Funny sort of job, yours.'

'You think so?' Willy did not seem anxious to be sociable.

They went upstairs to Willy's living-room, a large room elegantly proportioned, a remnant of the old house, with double doors, a marble mantelpiece and ornamental plaster ceiling. Willy's furniture was lost in it and a good deal of the space was taken up with trestle tables on which he had built a scale model of the Court. The houses, the verandahs, the yards and even the tree were all there. And the people. Outside each house the inhabitants were posed as if for a photograph. Bishop was intrigued.

'Christ! Is that me?'

'That was my intention.'

'Well, I'm damned! It's bloody marvellous. And there's Natalie sunbathing. What d'you do it for?'

'Fun,' Willy said. 'Now, Mr Bishop . . . '

Bishop fished in his wallet and came out with a letter. 'I had this from Crowther, the lawyer. It's a formal notice to quit when my lease on the Fenton Street property expires next year.'

He held out the letter to Willy but Willy did not take it. 'That is correct, Mr Bishop. I bought the property when your lease still had five years to run with an option of renewal for two. That period expires next year and I wish to put the premises to another use.'

'The hell you do!' Bishop sat down without being invited.

'Mr Crowther drew your attention to that possibility when you renewed, so it cannot have come as a surprise.'

Bishop fingered the sleek black hairs of his moustache. 'Of course, we are talking about money. Well, I don't mind admitting that the place suits me very well and while I have no intention of being a bloody milch cow for anybody, I'm willing to consider renewal at a fifteen per cent increase in rental.'

Willy shook his head.

'Fifteen per cent seems reasonable to me.'

'But as I do not intend to renew the lease, the question of rental does not arise.'

Bishop grinned. 'You're a hard man, Mr Goppel. All right, I might be prepared to stretch it a bit but twenty would be my absolute limit. Beyond that it would pay me to look somewhere else.'

'Which is what you will have to do in any case, Mr Bishop, if you wish to carry on your business.'

Bishop looked at him in astonishment. 'You bloody mean it, don't you?'

Willy did not answer.

'What have you got against me?'

'Against you? Nothing. I'm a business man, Mr Bishop, and I want to put that property to another use. Now you understand the position you will be able to make plans. I am sorry that Mr Crowther seems to have left you in some doubt.'

Bishop stood up. 'I don't give in that easy, Goppel. I've built up a business there and you aren't going to snatch the mat from under my bloody feet; don't you think it.'

Willy did not reply and after a moment, Bishop went on, 'What are you going to do with the place anyway?'

'That is my affair but you have my word that I shall not carry on a business similar to yours so you do not have to worry about competition.'

'Thank you for bloody nothing.'

'I'll see you out.'

*   *   *

The rainy windy weather continued through most of the week so that Natalie was not able to sunbathe on her verandah in the nude or otherwise, and Joan Fiske had no cause for complaint. But she had other worries and, on Thursday morning, seeking consolation and reassurance, she made an unprecedented visit to her neighbour, Mrs Hedley, who, it was said, was an initiate in the mysteries of the Tarot.

It was raining so hard that she had to take an umbrella even to go next door. Mrs Hedley received her with suspicion and kept her on the doorstep. Mrs Fiske was a little scared of the aristocratic and over-bearing old lady who, it was rumoured, had been to Roedean and Oxford in her day.

'I came because I happened to hear that you were an expert in the Tarot ... the Tarot, yes.' She had to repeat it twice before Mrs Hedley condescended to understand.

'Who told you that?'

'Actually I heard it in the greengrocer's but I can't remember who said it.'

Mrs Hedley yielded a point. 'I've done very little recently; what do you want?'

'I wondered if you would do a Reading for me?'

She received a shrewd, appraising look. 'I do not do it for money.'

'No, of course not.'

'And I do not do it for foolish women who merely want an idle pastime.'

Mrs Fiske flushed. 'No, I—'

'But if you have a problem, something which worries you, I don't mind seeing what the cards have to say about it.' Still she continued to block the door. 'You understand that I do not guarantee anything, sometimes it is necessary to undertake two or three Readings before a clear picture is achieved.'

'Of course.'

'Very well. You had better come in. Leave that umbrella outside, I don't want it dripping all over the place.'

In the living-room Mr Hedley was standing by the mantelpiece, a cigarette attached to his lower lip. He made a move to be hospitable but his wife cut him short.

'Mrs Fiske wants me to do a Reading for her, Herbert, so you had better go upstairs and lie down for a while.' She turned to her guest. 'You sit there, opposite me.' She pointed to a chair by the table then she went to a drawer in a mahogany chest and came back with a black silk square and a pack of cards. She placed the silk square in the middle of the table and carefully sorted the cards into two unequal piles. 'These are the Major and

Minor Arcana; if you don't know what that means, it doesn't matter. When is your birthday?'

'January the twenty-fifth.'

Now that Mrs Hedley was getting down to business her manner became more relaxed if not actually friendly.

'That means Aquarius; you should choose a court card from the Minor Arcana, suit of Swords.'

Joan Fiske fumbled inexpertly through the cards and came up with the Queen of Swords; the old lady smiled. She placed the card in the middle of the silk square. 'That is you; we call it the Significator.' She showed the other woman how to shuffle the cards in a special manner then, taking them from her, she laid down three of the Major Arcana above the Significator and followed with three rows of the Minor Arcana below the Significator.

There was silence in the room except for the sound of the downpour outside. The light was dim but Mrs Hedley did not switch on the lamp. Joan Fiske looked with dull curiosity at the colourful cards which, in some fashion, were supposed to hold something of herself and her problems. The old lady studied the cards, touching them, brooding over them and muttering to herself. Her grey eyes bulged slightly and with her sparse frizzled hair, her hooked nose and long bony hands, she would have made a good stand-in for a pantomime witch.

'You don't have to tell me what it is you want to know but it saves time.'

Joan Fiske's voice trembled. 'It's difficult.'

'It usually is.'

She hesitated a little longer then plunged. 'What with Marty and one thing and another I hardly know which way to turn . . . My husband has changed. He was never what you would call an easy man but lately I don't know where I am with him. He complains about what I spend on housekeeping then, in the very next breath, he grumbles that we haven't got this or that . . . ' She added after a moment with a certain coyness, 'We haven't slept in the same room for years.'

Mrs Hedley's silence seemed to encourage her.

'Last week when I had to go to Bristol for Marty's treatment I was away three days and he turned out the box-room and put a lot of things out for the dustman. Things you accumulate over the years – things which belonged to his father and to him as well as little things of mine. It seemed so cruel . . . I'm sure he *meant* to hurt me.'

Joan Fiske was near the end of her tether; several times her face moulded into a pathetic grimace, prelude to tears, but she controlled herself. 'Of course, he's six years younger than me.'

The old lady did not look up from the cards but said in a dry voice: 'So you haven't really got a specific question, my dear. Never mind, the cards may still help you. Forget about your husband for the moment. So many of our troubles come from within ourselves and can only be met with inner strength. This first line says something about you. Look – the Star, reversed . . . '

'Reversed?'

'Upside down, it alters the Reading. And on one side Force and on the other, the Hermit reversed.' Mrs Hedley pondered again. 'You lack confidence, confidence in others but especially in yourself. You are too pessimistic and you are disinclined to accept well meant advice and help . . . Against all that you have a great deal of moral courage and you are willing to suffer for what you believe to be right . . . You have the strength *to win through*.'

Joan Fiske listened as though she were hearing the

secrets of immortality and the old lady warmed to her work. 'You need to beware of judging by appearances; try to be more charitable. Bitterness harms you more than those against whom it is directed. Open your mind to fresh ideas . . . '

The Reading took half-an-hour and when it was over Joan Fiske, having achieved her catharis, was pathetically grateful. 'You've helped me enormously, Mrs Hedley. I would very much like to come again if I may.'

Mrs Hedley unbent. 'You will be welcome, my dear. You are an earnest Seeker. But do remember, so many of our problems are of our own making.'

The Wards had planned a rare break for the following week-end; they had arranged with the post office authorities for a Saturday stand-in and they were off to London for a hectic two days.

Henry had backed out.

On the Thursday they had their evening meal as usual and afterwards Henry took himself off to his room but Alison remained at the table with her parents. It was one of those evenings when the present seems curiously unreal and it is easy to sit doing nothing in a state of suspended animation.

'What *is* the matter with Henry, Alison?' Mrs Ward, unable to stay idle for long, shuffled plates together.

Alison was evasive. 'I don't know why you make such a fuss about him, mother; he gets spells when he's sorry for himself and that's all there is to it.'

'It's ever since he went to that woman's place; he goes round looking more miserable than I've ever seen him. I don't think he's doing his homework and he's not eating enough to keep a cat alive. Now he won't come with us to London.' She stopped rattling plates and looked at her daughter with great seriousness. I'm worried, Alison, really worried.'

Alison, because she too was a little concerned, pretended to an exasperation she did not feel. 'For goodness sake, mother, he's seventeen!'

'And she's well past thirty *and* she couldn't keep her husband so she's living with another man. I know her sort! What do you think, Edward?'

'Me? Oh, I agree with Alison; he's nearly a man and we've got to let him stand on his own feet.'

Henry's record player was churning out continuous jazz. Willy Goppel rarely suffered from nerves but this evening the insistent rhythm seemed to bite into his brain so that everything he did acquired a jerkiness like the movements of an automaton.

'The boy must be depressed,' Willy said, 'like me.'

Sergeant Kersey was planning an early night; he would spend a couple of hours watching television with the wife and kids or play Scrabble, or put a new catch on the bathroom door or bath the dog . . . A constable dropped a packet on his desk.

'What's that?'

'Just handed in at the desk, Sarge, addressed to you.'

It was an ordinary large-foolscap envelope addressed in neatly printed capitals, 'Detective Sergeant Kersey, Mallet Street Police Station'.

'Do you think it'll go bang if I open it?'

'I shouldn't think so, Sarge; everybody loves you.'

Kersey slit open the envelope and pulled out a thin wad of official looking papers, yellowing with age and creased through at the folds. He spread them out on his desk.

'They're all in German!' There was a photograph pasted on one of the documents impressed with an official stamp. 'Some poor kraut's papers from the last war. A captain by the look of it. Walter Pieck. Who the hell sent me this stuff? Who handed it in?'

'Dunno, Sarge. I just found it on the desk a few minutes ago.'

Kersey looked in the envelope once more and came up with a slip of paper on which there was a message printed in the same manner as the address on the envelope: 'These belong to Willy Goppel at Paul's Court.'

'Curiouser and curiouser.'

'Sarge?'

'I know this Willy Goppel, he makes dolls' houses and furniture for them. I wanted one for my girls when they were young but I couldn't afford it.' He gathered up the papers and stuffed them back in the envelope, 'I'll look in on Goppel on my way home.'

Kersey liked Falcon Street; it was a real city street, not one of those brash caverns stinking of exhaust fumes which often pass for streets in these days. There was more than a remnant of dignity about Falcon Street which, God knows why, had escaped the notice of planners and developers. Paul's Court was next to St Olave's Church which still had its graveyard with a few trees and shrubs, not too well cared for but none the worse for that.

'If I ever win the pools or get made up to chief D.I., I'll go for one of those houses in Paul's Court.'

Willy Goppel was fitting a gallery round the main landing of the dolls' house when Kersey came to the back door. Willy knew him by sight and felt uneasy.

'You remember me, Mr Goppel? Detective Sergeant Kersey.'

'Yes, I remember you.' Willy resumed work on the gallery, not as a discourtesy but when his hands were busy he felt more at ease.

Kersey lit a cigarette and watched. When the fitting was complete he sighed. 'I wish I could do work like that.'

Willy allowed his apprehension to peep through. 'Something has happened?'

But the policeman had moved over to the animal cages and was standing by them, his back to Willy. 'Look at that!' He was pointing to one of the geckos walking upside down on the glass roof of its cage. 'Clever, that.'

'He has adhesive pads on his feet. Now, Sergeant, you wish to ask me something?'

'Nothing much. Some anonymous joker sent me these with a note saying they belong to you.' Kersey spread the papers on Willy's work bench.

Although he had known what was coming Willy felt a hollowness inside. 'That is correct, they are mine.'

'This chap, Walter Pieck – was he a friend of yours?'

'I was Walter Pieck, Sergeant.' Willy had made up his mind that he would not lie.

'Was?'

'I *am* Walter Pieck, if you prefer it.' Willy spoke with dignity.

'Me? I don't care one way or the other. All I want to do is to get home to my supper. You lost these?'

'Yes.'

'Dropped them in the street?'

'No, they were taken from that desk over there while I was out.'

'Don't you lock up when you go out?'

'I do now.'

'Did you report it to the police?'

'No.'

'Anything else taken?'

'Some money and a string of medals. They were all together in a cigar box.'

'Why should whoever took them send this stuff to me?'

'I have no idea, Sergeant.'

Willy was by no means reassured by the policeman's easy, almost indifferent manner. He knew all about the soft sell.

'Sounds a bit screwy to me.' Kersey was picking up

fittings for the dolls' house, looking at them and putting them down again. 'I suppose you thought it would be easier to get British citizenship if you didn't apply as an ex-infantry captain. I expect you were right at that. Now you probably wish you'd stayed a Deutscher.'

Willy said, 'I took the identity of a dead man – Willy Goppel.'

'It must have been a hell of a long time ago.'

'Spring 1945.'

Kersey shrugged. 'I should think they'd look on you as a paid-up member by now.' He folded the papers and replaced them in the envelope. 'You've got no record?'

'With the police? No.'

'I don't suppose you killed this chap Goppel?'

'I did not. He was a *Sklavenarbeiter* – what you call a slave worker, a German Jew, and he died in an accident. He must have had some skill they valued or he would not have lived so long . . . '

Willy broke off. He had a sudden clear vision of a sunny country road, a sandy bank gouged out by a truck which must have careered down the hill out of control. The truck lay on its side and strewn about like rag dolls were four bodies. One of them, Willy thought, looked vaguely like him . . . What he remembered most clearly was the stillness, the sunlit silence which was almost tangible. Yet there was enemy armour across the river.

'I took a dead man's clothes and papers.'

'Have you still got his papers?'

'No, I destroyed them years ago.'

'But kept your own.'

Willy was silent. What was the use of trying to explain?

Kersey sighed. 'I shall have to send these to the Home Office but unless there's somebody there tired of sitting on his arse I doubt if you'll hear any more.'

The sergeant's words were probably meant kindly but they brought Willy no consolation. He felt that he had been stripped naked – more, that he had lost a protective skin.

'Where did your wife come into all this?'

Willy took his time. 'This was Germany in the spring of nineteen forty-five. Even before I changed my clothes with a dead man I was a deserter. I had failed to rejoin my regiment in the east after convalescent leave . . . I was making my way west with just what I could carry in a haversack.

'Just before the war I had moved with my parents and sister to Essen and all three were killed in the bombing of the Ruhr . . . ' He broke off and wiped his forehead with a red handkerchief. 'I am not excusing myself; I do not feel the need to do so to anyone who did not share the experiences of those last days . . . Anyway, within a few hours of changing clothes with the man, Goppel, I was wounded while trying to cross the river – hit by a stray bullet. I was picked up, unconscious, by a British patrol and taken to a British field hospital where my future wife was a nurse . . . I had on my person only the papers of the dead man but foolishly, perhaps with the cowardly notion of not committing myself, I had kept my own papers in the haversack with a few souvenirs. When I recovered consciousness in hospital I hoped and believed that the haversack had been lost in the river.'

Willy resumed work on the landing of the dolls' house, fitting more balusters into their tiny drilled holes. 'It was long afterwards, when we were married and settled here, that my wife returned to me my haversack and its contents which she had kept along with my secret.'

Kersey said, 'It's all a long time ago.' He glanced at his watch. 'I must be off. *Viel Glück!*'

Willy did not smile.

44

CHAPTER THREE

By Saturday the rain had gone, it was a sunny warm day and the weathermen had promised a fine week-end. Henry Ward got out of bed after a troubled, restless night. Alone in the house for two whole days he had no idea what he would do with himself. His parents and Alison had taken the night train to London and he thought of them now, breakfasting in their hotel, and wished that he was with them. He had stayed home in order to make his peace with Yvette – not that he felt deeply drawn to her but he had treated her badly and he wanted to salve his conscience. Henry hated to hurt people, but more than that he hated loose ends; he had a tidy mind.

He put on his dressing-gown, switched on the radio, made some instant coffee and took it into the living-room where he stood by the window, gazing down into the Court. Marty Fiske was there, going round and round the oak tree, lost in some vague, mysterious private world. Natalie Cole's red sports-car was parked nearby.

'If she crooked her finger I should still go running.'

He ground his teeth, hating himself.

Yvette was coming down the verandah steps from her house, wearing the eternal T-shirt and jeans. He would have gone down to her but he wasn't dressed. He watched her cross the Court and go into Willy Goppel's, presumably to help him with his animals. Perhaps he could catch her when she came out.

But he missed her. The day wore on. Out of the

mounds of food his mother had left him he heated a small meat pie and had it for lunch. After lunch he played records, keeping an eye on the Court in case Yvette should go out again.

At about half-past three he heard the engine of the little sports-car roar into life and he hurried to the window. Natalie was in the car alone. She looked up and saw him, grinned and waved. It meant less than nothing to her. He wondered how she thought of it – if she thought of it at all . . . 'A bit of fun with the Ward boy . . . Teaching the Ward boy a few tricks . . .' Or perhaps she expressed herself more crudely. He squirmed.

He supposed that Yvette would be in the house alone and he had almost made up his mind to go there when it occurred to him that Bishop might be home on a Saturday afternoon. He was still trying to decide whether or not to risk it when he saw Yvette coming out of the house. She had her shoulder bag so, presumably, she was going out. He ran down the two flights of stairs. Locking up delayed him and by the time he got to Falcon Street Yvette was nowhere to be seen. It was not surprising for the market people were packing up their cars and vans and the skeletons of their stalls were everywhere. He decided that Yvette would make for the city centre and hared off up the street to the bus stop but he was too late; he saw her get on the bus but he was too far away. He set out on foot.

He was in a strange mood; it was suddenly imperative that he should find her and talk to her. He thought that it should not be too difficult if he made the rounds of the coffee bars and discos.

As he arrived in the centre the clock over the town hall was chiming a quarter past four. Too early for the discos, so he wandered around more or less aimlessly peering into every coffee bar he came to and entering those he could not see into from the outside. In consequence he got involved with some of his school friends.

'Have you seen Yvette?'

'Oi! Oi! What's going on, then? Somebody looking for something they shouldn't. That's for sure.'

It was strange; whenever Yvette's name was mentioned somebody was sure to insinuate that she was easy. In fact, when he had been out with her she had not been like that at all. They had never got further than mild petting and whenever he had shown signs of doing more it was, 'Give it a rest, Henry . . . Lay off! What do you think I am?'

By six o'clock he had drunk several cups of coffee and got nowhere and he was beginning to feel ridiculous. The discos were opening and he promised himself that he would try one or two before giving up and going home. He had been walking more or less at random, making wide circuits round the city centre, and it happened that he was now in Hilary Street, a quiet backwater where former warehouses had been converted into antique shops, picture galleries, book shops and offices for architects and surveyors. There was only one other person in the street and it was Yvette. She was walking along the pavement ahead of him with short quick steps, her bag slung from her shoulder. He had started to hurry when she turned down a flight of steps to some basement; a door opened and she was gone.

The building was the Hilary Street Arts Centre but a neon sign with a downwardly pointing arrow indicated that the basement was The Catacombs, a restaurant. He went down the steps to a white enamelled door with a glass panel and polished brass fittings. A notice read, 'Closed. Open from six-thirty for dinners.' A brass-framed menu was fastened to the wall by the door. Expensive.

*

Willy had been feeling unwell all day, now his skin was dry and hot, his face burned, his throat was constricted and prickly and his arms and legs felt incredibly heavy.

'I must have a temperature.'

Like hundreds of others in the city Willy had contracted summer influenza. The newspapers spoke of a new and more virulent form which was especially dangerous to the old and those in late middle-age. He sat in his chair, staring into the empty fireplace, sometimes drifting off into a doze then waking with a start. When he dozed he seemed to be Walter Pieck again, twenty seven years old, re-living those last traumatic days in Germany. But things went differently. When, for example, he bent over the corpse of Willy Goppel he saw not a face but a skull, and when he started to unbutton the man's tunic to exchange clothes, hundreds of fat, pale-yellow maggots swarmed and writhed in an unspeakable cavity where the chest should have been.

The musical chimes of the black marble clock on the mantelpiece brought him back; it chimed the hour and struck eight, he counted the strokes. He rarely drank spirits but he kept a bottle of whisky in the house and he wondered if a glass might do him good. He was still wondering when the shop doorbell rang. His first reaction was to let it ring but the visitor was persistent and in the end he went slowly downstairs and opened the door. It was the Professor, come to tell him of his enquiries into the theft of Willy's papers and medals. They went upstairs together and Willy fetched the whisky from a cupboard in the kitchen. The effort of moving about made him feel better for a time but when he was back in his chair the feverish symptoms returned and now his heart seemed to be beating much faster than usual.

'You are ill, my friend.'

The Professor sat talking away but Willy scarcely

heard what he had to say though he gathered that the enquiries had met with little success.

'In the circumstances I should try to forget about your loss, my dear Willy, I doubt whether you will see your papers again.'

Willy hadn't the strength to tell him that they were already in the hands of the police. He only wished that the Professor would go.

'You need medicine, my friend. Can I get you anything? Don't you think I should telephone for the doctor?'

Willy put him off. 'The girl from next door is getting a prescription made up for me; she will be bringing it in later this evening.'

In the end, when the Professor was leaving, Willy asked him to let himself out through the back. 'The door is unlocked and it will save me coming down.'

'You wish the door to remain unlocked – is that wise?'

'Until Yvette comes with my medicine. I usually lock up when I go to bed.'

The Professor was gone at last. Willy looked at the black marble clock, it was ten minutes past nine. His friend had meant well but he had stayed too long and the whisky had made Willy's head worse. Yvette had promised to have the medicine made up for him at a chemist's; it was a prescription he had had by him for years and he used it whenever he had influenza or a heavy cold.

'I shan't be back until late but I'll be sure to get it made up before they close.'

He wondered vaguely what she had meant by 'late'. It was very quiet, no traffic in Falcon Street and the Wards were away except for Henry. Henry must be out or he would be playing his record player or listening to the radio. It was so silent that he felt muffled in cottonwool and wondered if his hearing was affected . . .

He must have dozed again for he was back in Germany, this time as a boy. He was in bed, lying prone, and he could see the high wooden foot of the bed. It was of some dark wood, elaborately carved with fruit and flowers. He was aware of his mother, a vague figure standing by the bed and she was saying something which, try as he would, he could not hear.

*   *   *

On Sunday morning the city looked as though it had been desolated by the plague. On what would probably be the last summer Sunday of the year half the population had joined an exodus to coast and moor.

Joan Fiske was giving Marty his breakfast; her husband was still in bed. Marty sat at the plastic-topped table in the kitchen shovelling cornflakes into his mouth with a spoon held in his fist. The kitchen window was open to the yard and a shaft of sunlight just reached the stainless steel sink making it shine like polished silver. The air was warm and fresh and balmy with the promise of a glorious day. But Joan Fiske was uneasy, her visit to Mrs Hedley and the Tarot had calmed her and she was making a determined effort to come to terms with her problems but on this sunny morning melancholy had stolen up on her unawares. She who had resolutely refused to remember the past was assailed by nostalgia; for a time before marriage; before Marty.

She looked at her son and sighed then immediately felt guilty. Marty triumphantly scooped up the last drop of milk and pushed his bowl away, then he reached into his pocket and began to take things out and put them on the table. A piece of string, an oddly shaped stone, a clothes peg, a dirty handkerchief and then a lady's watch, on a bracelet made up of lucky charms.

'Marty! Where did you get that?'

Marty looked at his mother in blank incomprehension.

'The watch, Marty – where did you get it? Tell me, Marty, it's important. . . '

It was one of her nightmares that Marty might take up to steal.

Marty merely lifted the watch to his ear, shook it and listened. His mother snatched it from him. 'Marty—' She broke off, hearing heavy footsteps on the stairs. 'There's your father. It doesn't matter now.' She slipped the watch into the pocket of her housecoat. 'Put all that stuff away, Marty! Do you hear me?'

The door opened and Martin Fiske came in looking sullen and heavy eyed. He wore a mauve dressing-gown over his pyjamas. 'Hasn't he had his breakfast yet? What's all that rubbish?'

'Collect up your things, Marty. You can go out into the Court, it's a lovely day.'

The Hedleys had been up for hours and had reached the stage of morning coffee which they drank from pottery mugs. Mrs Hedley said, 'I shall make a ginger cake.'

'But we don't eat ginger cake.'

'Toby does.'

'What's that got to do with it? He hasn't been near us for months.'

'All the same, I have a feeling. I shall make that cake . . . '

Henry Ward got out of bed at the start of another day on his own.

Willy Goppel was not around.

Natalie Cole rolled over to face the man who shared her bed. She slid one arm round his neck and pressed her body against his. 'Come on, Geoff, for Christ's sake.'

Bishop remained supine and unresponsive. 'Not this morning, I'm not up to it.'

'What's the matter? Are you ill or something? It's that bloody garage, worrying about the lease. There are other premises for God's sake!'

Bishop made an angry movement. 'Lay off, Natalie!'

Natalie whisked back the bedclothes and put her feet over the side; she was naked. ' "La Cass" isn't exactly a bloody picnic these days but I don't bring my troubles home with me. Anyway, it's half-ten, do you want any coffee?'

'If you like.'

'I don't care a damn one way or the other. It isn't exactly a privilege to wait on you.'

Bishop sat up in bed and grabbed her by the wrist. 'I told you to lay off!'

She squirmed round to face him in a sudden rage, 'And if I don't?'

He let go of her wrist and mumbled something.

'What was that?'

'I said, I feel lousy this morning. I was pissed last night.'

'Poor you! You should give up screwing that slut in your office then you might manage to be a man for me when I need one.'

She got off the bed and, still naked, went into the bathroom leaving the door open.

He heard her turn on the shower.

'What time did you get home last night, Geoff?'

'About midnight. Why?'

'Did you see Yvette?'

'No, she must've been in bed.'

When she had finished in the bathroom Natalie put on a wrap and went down to the kitchen. She put coffee in the percolator and switched it on. There was no milk in the refrigerator so she went to the front

52

door to bring in the morning delivery. To her surprise the door was still bolted; usually Yvette would have been out long before. She called from the bottom of the stairs, 'Yvette! Are you still in bed?'

There was no answer so she went up to the girl's room; the bed was empty and unmade. Natalie was concerned. There was a sideway out of the house through the yard and into the Court but it was never used, and in any case the kitchen door was still bolted from the inside.

She shouted, 'Geoff! Yvette didn't come home last night.'

There was an incomprehensible reply and she called again but it was some time before Bishop came downstairs in his dressing-gown. He was a big man, in his late thirties, with a black moustache which drooped at the ends.

'I'm going to phone the police, Geoff.'

'I shouldn't be in too much of a hurry. Yvette can take care of herself.'

'When did you last see her?'

Bishop frowned. 'I don't think I saw her all day yesterday.'

Natalie said, 'She was with me about lunchtime, we had something together out of a tin. I left her here around three and went into town for a hair appointment; after that it was straight on to La Cass.'

'She's probably spent the night with one of her mates; she'll ring up directly.'

'To hell with that!' Natalie went to the telephone and made a 999 call. She sounded rattled, which was unusual. 'They're going to send somebody.' She went into the kitchen and poured coffee. 'She's been bloody-minded this past few days.'

'You think she might have taken herself off somewhere?'

53

'It's possible.' An idea occurred to her. 'If she has she'll have taken her clothes.' Natalie went upstairs and was gone some time; when she came down she looked more worried. 'As far as I can tell she only had what she stood up in, jeans and a T-shirt – what she was wearing yesterday morning.'

Bishop stood by the sink, his bottom propped against the drainer. Once or twice he started to say something but changed his mind.

She paused in front of him. 'You haven't been trying it on again with her?'

Bishop raised his eyes ceilingwards. 'God! You aren't going to let me forget that! It was just that once. I was drunk, and anyway I didn't do anything to the kid.'

Natalie shrugged.

Bishop said, 'When the cops come they'll ask a hell of a lot of questions.'

'So?'

'I shouldn't say anything to them about that. It was months ago.'

'I don't suppose you're the first bastard to try it on with a fifteen-year-old girl living in the same house.'

'All the same, better not say anything. I've got form remember.'

Natalie rounded on him. 'You make me sick!'

'But you won't say anything?'

'No, I'll draw a picture.'

They heard a car in the Court and Natalie went to the door. 'Oh, it's you.' Sergeant Kersey followed her in.

'What's all this, then? I happened to be this way and they got me on my car radio.'

'Yvette has been missing since sometime yesterday.'

'So they said. What will she be now – fourteen? Fifteen?'

'Fifteen.'

'Same age as my eldest.' Kersey took a packet of

cigarettes from his pocket and lit one absently, eyeing the decor. 'I heard you were living in one of these.'

He was no stranger to Bishop or Natalie. Banger Bishop's Car Mart and Vehicle Hire had been the scene of one or two punch-ups and Bishop himself had been convicted on a wounding charge. By the same token nightclubs are regarded as high-risk places and the police make it their business to know who runs them.

Kersey asked obvious questions and got obvious answers. He could have written the scenario himself.

'Would you say that she had any reason to run away?'

'No.'

'No rows? No tantrums? You know what kids are when they get upset.'

'No rows or tantrums.'

'Boy-friend?'

'Nobody special.'

'Have you noticed anything different about her lately?'

'No, nothing.'

'Have you enquired from the neighbours?'

'What's it got to do with them?'

Kersey dropped ash into an eviscerated glass swan which happened to be handy. 'You haven't seen Yvette since yesterday afternoon, they might have.'

'I hadn't thought of that. I'll have a word.'

'Better leave it to us now.'

Natalie was uncomfortable. Without saying much Kersey was making her feel guilty of something.

'I shall want a list of people she might visit – relatives, friends, school pals . . . ' He stood in front of one of the green and blue pictures, scowling at it. 'Are there any other kids in the Court?'

'Only the Wards at the post office; they have a boy and a girl but I think they're away for the weekend.'

'How old?'

'The girl is about the same age as Yvette but the boy is older.'

'Have you got a recent photograph?'

'She had one taken at school last term.'

'I expect that will do. Now, one more question – is it possible that Yvette has gone off with or to her father?'

Natalie looked surprised. 'I never even thought of it! They wouldn't know each other if they met in the street. It's ten or twelve years—'

'All the same, can you help us to locate him?'

'I'm not sure; the last I heard he was living in Lincoln but that must have been four or five years back.'

'Right! Now I'd like to see her room.'

Bishop said with apparent relief, 'You don't want me?'

'I shouldn't think so; not at the moment anyway.'

'I'll get along then, I'm due at the garage . . . '

Natalie led the way upstairs to a bedroom at the back of the house. It was a pleasant enough room with built-in units – wardrobe, dressing-table, desk and wash-basin. There was a divan bed which was unmade. A transistor radio on a ledge above the bed rubbed shoulders with a china cat and a framed photograph of some pop-star.

'You can't go by the bed,' Natalie said, 'she often doesn't make it until she's going to get in it again and sometimes not then.'

A shelf above the desk held a few school books, textbooks and exercise books all jumbled together. Kersey flicked through one of the exercise books and found it liberally annotated in red ink with critical comments.

'She hates school,' Natalie said.

In the wardrobe there were several pairs of jeans, a drawer full of T-shirts, and another of a random collection of briefs, bras, and stockings all stuffed in together; three or four dresses, a couple of school blazers and skirts were draped on hangers.

Kersey looked in the drawers of the desk but there seemed to be nothing of interest – two or three ballpoint pens, a writing pad and some envelopes. In the deeper, bottom drawer there was a bundle of magazines of the sort that are published for not very bright teenaged girls. He lifted them out and underneath there was a shallow tin box that had once held shortbread biscuits. In it there was a little diary of the engagement type and eighteen five-pound notes.

Natalie said, 'Good God! Where did she get all that money? Not from me, that's for sure!'

Kersey flicked through the pages of the diary, most of which were blank. Where there was an entry it consisted of initials, a cabalistic sign or a single word. Kersey passed it to Natalie.

'Do the initials mean anything to you?'

Natalie looked at the book and shook her head. 'I don't really know any of her friends, she never brings anybody home and she's the secretive type.' After a pause she added, 'I wish I knew where she got that money. You don't think she's been going with men?'

Irritation got the better of Kersey, 'How the hell should I know?' Then in his usual manner he went on, 'I'll take the diary, the initials might give us a lead.'

They went downstairs together. 'I'll make a few enquiries round the Court before I go back to the nick so if you get any messages for me, or if you hear from Yvette . . . Before I go you'd better give me some idea of who's who in the Court.'

She did so.

'What can I do?'

'Not much, I'm afraid; just be around in case she comes back or gets in touch.'

He left with a school photograph of Yvette and a description dictated by her mother.

Kersey had two daughters of his own – one thirteen,

the other fifteen. They were good kids but you could never be sure. He put in a good deal of time worrying about them. Occasionally, though not often, he wished that they were boys. You knew where you were with boys. As a cop he knew it all from the inside, the young tart who high-tails it off to London to sell her wares in a better market; the starry eyed innocent who, hand in hand with her soppy boy-friend, steals away into the sunset to find it dark, cold and wet; and the poor little devil who is just unlucky enough to catch the eye of some pervert and end up in a ditch, very dead.

Growing up in New Guinea, Coming of Age in Samoa, Male and Female . . . Kersey knew his Margaret Mead, and he'd dipped into Malinowski, Linton and Coon before coming to the conclusion that there are few so-called primitive societies where the business of growing up is so hazardous and cruel as is our own, where there is so little order and less discipline but an unrestricted freedom to go to the devil.

And it was a bad start to have Natalie as a mother. Her most engaging attributes did not make her apt for motherhood. Of course, the kid might turn up at any minute saying the boyfriend's bike had run out of petrol. Or she might not. The real question was whether she had gone away of her own accord or been persuaded. There was an even better question, whether she was alive or dead.

Coming up for Sunday lunchtime; nobody would be pleased to see him but it couldn't be helped. He stood by his car, taking in the lay-out. Goppel's place was to the left of the archway coming in, the Wards' and their post office to the right. Natalie's house on the right and the Fiskes' at the far end were separated by a corner garden plot, shared between the two houses. The Hedleys', on the left of the Court, had no garden because the garages were on that side. Between the

58

garages and Goppel's yard there was a small iron gate which gave access to Church Lane, a pedestrian path which linked Falcon Street with parallel Church Street. The oak tree, which Kersey greatly admired, stood in the middle of the Court.

In the Fiskes' garden a man was burning rubbish in a patent incinerator. He was tall, fortyish, and his cardigan bulged slightly with a developing paunch. He worked with meticulous detachment in the manner of a man unused to such menial tasks. A column of grey-brown smoke rose in the still air, well clear of the houses, before it was caught by cross currents and whisked away.

Mr Hedley answered the door after Kersey had been ringing for some time. If it had not been for the sound of the radio he would have assumed that they were out. Hedley was very tall, very lean and pale as though he had been grown in semi-darkness, and he had a ragged, grey moustache stained with nicotine.

'What's it all about?'

'If I could come in . . . '

He was taken into the living-room where Mrs Hedley, a female counterpart of her husband though cast in a more aristocratic mould, was seated at the table in the dining alcove. He was impressed by an air of cultured if somewhat tarnished and dusty elegance; the Bechstein grand, shelves of musical scores, hundreds of books, two or three pieces of good furniture and a faded carpet of Chinese silk. Though the meal of stew he was interrupting looked unappetizing, the silver, china and glass on the table had never seen the inside of a chain-store.

'Don't let me interrupt your meal.'

Hedley took his seat opposite his wife while the radio continued to blare out Sibelius's fifth. He jerked a fork in the direction of the radio. 'That's Sibelius. Do you know, the Finnish Government passed a special law so that he could get his booze.' The old man chuckled. Clearly this was his favourite music story.

Kersey asked if the volume might be turned down.

'What does he want?' Mrs Hedley demanded of her husband.

'He wants the radio turned down.'

'Turn it off, then. I can't hear with all this going on anyway.'

Hedley switched off the set.

'Yvette Cole is missing. Her mother hasn't seen her since yesterday lunchtime.'

Mrs Hedley made a disdainful sound. 'That comes as no surprise, I doubt if she knows where the child is half the time.'

'She didn't come home last night.'

'She's a whore.'

'The child?'

'I was referring to the mother, I know nothing of the child.'

'Can either of you remember when you last saw Yvette?'

Mr Hedley said, 'I saw her yesterday afternoon.'

'At what time, approximately?'

'I was having a smoke on the verandah, it must have been between three and four.'

Mrs Hedley put in, 'My husband's memory is unreliable.'

'Was she alone?'

'I didn't see anybody with her. She came out of the house and crossed the Court. I think she went through the arch out into Falcon Street.'

'Can you say how she was dressed?'

'Of course he can't!'

Mr Hedley ignored his wife.

'She had on those tight trouser things young people

60

wear and a white jumper with letters on it – she always dresses like that except when she's going to school.'

'Was there anybody in the Court at the time?'

'Only Marty Fiske and he's retarded.'

Mrs Hedley said, 'In my day we should have called him an idiot and he'd have been none the worse for that. He's harmless.'

'So neither of you saw anything unusual on Saturday?'

They agreed that they had not.

'I understand that the people from the post office are away?'

'Not the boy, he didn't go.'

Hedley looked at his wife in surprise. 'Are you sure?'

'Of course I'm sure, I saw him in their yard this morning.' She turned to Kersey, 'He's another of that woman's conquests and she almost old enough to be his mother.'

Her husband was mildly shocked. 'You've no reason to say that, Emmie; the boy is a friend of Yvette's . . . '

The old lady laughed. 'You said yourself that he was there for two hours last Sunday afternoon when the man she lives with was out and so was Yvette.'

'Yes, but that doesn't mean—'

'It does with her.'

Kersey thought that he had got all that he could hope for so, apologizing once more, he left them to their lunch and the radio.

When he had gone Hedley paused with his fork half-way to his mouth.

'What's the matter now?'

'I've just remembered what I saw on Saturday night – I told you—'

'You imagined it.'

'But I tell you—'

'You said he was coming out of Willy Goppel's.'

'I said I thought he was.'

'You *thought*!'

They ate in silence for a while then Hedley said, 'Do you think we ought to have a word with Toby about this?'

'Why?'

'Well, the police might go to see him.'

'Why should they? In any case we can tell him when he comes over this afternoon.'

For the first time Hedley betrayed impatience. 'You know damn well he isn't coming this afternoon. You just imagine these things.'

'And I'm usually right.'

The old man sighed and resumed his meal. After a little while Mrs Hedley said, 'Turn on the radio, we are missing the concert.'

Natalie called across to Kersey as he left the Hedleys. 'They want you to telephone the nick.'

He telephoned from a box outside the post office and spoke to his immediate superior, Inspector Ware.

'What's happening, Doug?'

'I don't know yet; the girl's been missing since yesterday afternoon but whether she went off on her tod or was picked up I haven't a clue.'

Ware was young with every intention of rising fast. 'She's under age, we can't afford to pussy-foot around on this one.'

'Nobody's pussy-footing. I'm making enquiries among the people who know her. I've got a photo and description so if you like to send a patrol car to pick 'em up you can have 'em on the telex straight away.'

'I'll do that but I think we might have to off-load this one, Doug. Twenty-four hours is a long time for a kid to be missing before anybody gets a finger out.'

'That's up to you.'

'It's Natalie's girl, isn't it?'

'It is.'

'And Natalie is living with Banger Bishop – right?'

'You've been doing your homework – sir.'

'You know Bishop was sent down for G.B.H. three years ago?'

'Yes, Bishop is a dyed-in-the-wool villain and we'll trip him up one of these days but that doesn't mean he's after young girls.'

'He drew a knife on a chap.'

'I know he did, it was me who nicked him but what's that got to do with it?'

'I don't trust him. I'm going to have a word with the super.'

'No skin off my nose.'

'Okay, Doug, keep in touch.'

After a troubled night, when it was already daylight, Henry had fallen into a deep sleep and he did not wake until well past eleven. As soon as he regained conscious-ness he was aware of an underlying uneasiness, then he recalled his encounter with Yvette the night before. He felt that he had made matters worse. He got out of bed and drew the curtains. There was a strange car parked outside the Coles', an Escort which had seen better days. Why hadn't he gone to London with the family? He put on his dressing-gown and went downstairs. It was a beautiful day but he could think of nothing that he wanted to do. Somebody was ringing the back-door bell.

He went down to the ground floor and unlocked the door.

'Henry Ward?'

The man was not as tall as Henry but more heavily built and he wore a grey suit which looked as though it had been around for a long time. 'I'm Detective Sergeant Kersey. I want to talk to you. Can I come in?'

Henry had reached the age of seventeen without ever

63

being questioned by a policeman and he was apprehensive. He led the way through the office-store behind the shop and upstairs to the living-room.

'Haven't you got a room of your own?'

'Yes, of course, but what do you want to talk to me about?'

'Yvette Cole. So you didn't go to London with your parents?'

Henry was shaken by this evidence of inside knowledge. 'What about Yvette? Has something happened to her?'

'Why didn't you go to London?'

Henry, on edge, nervous, and exasperated by the sergeant's manner, burst out: 'What the hell does that matter? I'm asking you about Yvette?'

The policeman's face became wooden. 'Correction! I'm asking you about Yvette. Now, what about this room of yours?'

He would have liked to refuse but he hadn't the nerve. On the next landing he said, 'That is my sister's room, this is mine. Do you want to search it?'

Henry had meant to be sarcastic and he was shocked when the policeman started looking through his books and shuffling through his records. 'I see you've got some seventy-eights.'

'I collect jazz records. What's happened to Yvette?'

'That's what we'd all like to know. When did you last see her?'

He compromised with the truth. 'I saw her on Friday at school.'

'When did you last go out together?'

'It must be more than a week ago.'

'A quarrel?'

Now the sergeant was opening drawers and glancing through their contents as though it was the most natural thing in the world.

'I don't think you have any right to pry into my things like that.'

Kersey looked at him as though mildly surprised. 'No right at all. Do you object? Got something to hide? I was told that you are fairly close to Yvette and, naturally, I want to know what sort of bloke you are.'

He went on snapping laconic questions and at the same time conducting a fairly comprehensive search of the room.

'Does Yvette go round with other boys?'

'She has done; one or two, but she isn't a tart if that's what you mean.'

Kersey said, 'You went to her house last Sunday afternoon and spent a couple of hours there but Yvette was out and so, incidentally, was Geoff Bishop. Just you and Natalie. You said that it's more than a week since you went out with Yvette, did you go there in the hope of meeting her?'

Henry felt himself flushing and looked away. 'Mrs Cole invited me over for a drink because I'd helped her one morning when she couldn't start her car.'

'She was grateful?'

'I suppose so.'

'How grateful? Did she let you take her to bed?'

Henry felt outclassed; the policeman seemed to be playing with him and at any moment . . .'

'Come on, lad; you're not talking to your maiden aunt and I know Natalie.'

'All right, she did. Is it illegal?'

'No, and it might do you more good than harm if you don't try to make a habit of it. The point is, did Yvette find out?'

Henry could not find words.

'Did she? Out with it!'

He nodded. 'She came in just as I was coming downstairs.'

The sergeant whistled. 'That's bad! You had a row?'

'No, she wouldn't talk.' He paused for a moment, trying to fathom the policeman's mind. 'You are not saying that's why she's gone away?'

'How should I know?'

At that point Henry would gladly have told the sergeant all he knew, but he had promised. He perched himself on the arm of a chair trying to appear relaxed but looking instead like a sullen schoolboy in trouble. The policeman stood over him.

'I suppose you want her found?'

'Of course I do!'

'Then I'll tell you what you're going to do; you're going to make a list of every boy, girl, man and woman who meant anything to Yvette. I mean, by that, anybody who was more than just an acquaintance. Try to remember the people she talked about; it doesn't matter whether you know them or not.'

'I'll try.' He began to feel better at the prospect of having something to do.

Kersey seemed to lose interest in him. 'I'm going to talk to Willy Goppel.'

'I think he's away. I haven't seen him or heard him and he often does go away overnight at week-ends.'

'Relatives?'

'I don't think so. As far as I know his only relative is his son who lives close by. – somewhere near the pannier market. He shares a flat with Toby Lennon.'

'Who's he?'

'He's Mrs Hedley's nephew, he used to live with them here in the Court.'

Kersey left the Wards' house and went out into Falcon Street. A police car was parked down the street and two uniformed men were ringing doorbells: Inspector Ware leaving no stone unturned; but it was an unprofitable occupation for a Sunday afternoon for most people were out in their cars. He decided to talk to the Fiskes.

The promptitude with which Mrs Fiske answered the door suggested that she must have been watching for him. He was shown into the living-room where Mr Fiske, the man he had seen burning rubbish in the garden, was reading the *Sunday Telegraph*.

'Come in, Sergeant! Can I offer you something?' Expansive and pompous.

'You know why I'm here?'

Fiske said, 'We saw the commotion and I stepped across the Court to enquire.'

Joan Fiske sat on the edge of her chair, her hands gripping each other in her lap. She was the pale, lean, nervous complement of her husband's suave pomposity. 'It's not that we are inquisitive but it seemed only neighbourly.'

Fiske adopted a man-to-man approach. 'I doubt if we can be of much help, but if there is anything we can tell you, needless to say . . . ' He shifted in his chair. 'You see, Sergeant, one doesn't want to gossip but if Yvette has run away it's not altogether surprising. I doubt if she even remembers her father, and her mother is fully occupied with her business. I'm not suggesting that she was in any way ill-treated but she probably felt to some extent neglected – overlooked.'

'When did you last see Yvette?'

Mrs Fiske frowned. 'We don't really take a lot of interest in our neighbours; I really couldn't tell you the last time I saw her.'

Kersey was puzzled, not by this suburban housewife line but by why, in this instance, it was accompanied by such evident tension. Mrs Fiske was making a great effort to control herself but when she spoke her voice trembled and even her husband looked at her in surprise.

Fiske said, 'I don't know when she went missing but it occurs to me that I saw her yesterday afternoon.'

67

'You weren't home yesterday afternoon, so how could you have seen her?'

Fiske went on as though his wife had not spoken. 'Although it was Saturday I went back to the office after lunch. I am an accountant with offices in King Street and it happened that I saw Yvette from my office window, walking along the other side of the street.'

'Alone?'

'Yes.'

'Carrying anything?'

'Nothing obvious, she might have had a handbag or something of the sort.'

'How was she dressed?'

'The usual T-shirt and jeans.'

'Going towards or away from the city centre?'

'Oh, towards the centre.'

'Any idea of time?'

Fiske considered. 'It must have been about four o'clock, give or take fifteen minutes.'

Kersey stood up. 'Thank you, Mr Fiske, that could be useful; it shows that she went into town after her mother left.'

Mrs Fiske was on her feet, ready to see him out. 'And it means that whatever happened to her didn't happen here. That centre is becoming a jungle!' Pleased with the phrase, she repeated it, 'A jungle!' She edged him towards the door. 'It's not safe to go through there in the evenings and I blame those West Indians, it wasn't like it before they came.'

Kersey was on the point of leaving when the door opened and Marty shambled in. He looked from one to another, grinned, and mumbled something about his watch.

'Not now, Marty!' His mother's voice was sharp. 'You can see we've got a visitor.' She turned to Kersey,

'This is our son, Marty, Mr Kersey. He's a little . . . You understand.'

Before leaving the Court Kersey rang Willy Goppel's doorbell but there was no response. He drove back to Mallet Street station in his little Escort which had already clocked up eighty thousand miles of hard driving and was beginning to sound like it. He had his paper-work to do, then it was almost certain that the big boys would take over and after that all he would hear of the case would be from station gossip and what he read in the newspapers. He sat at his desk, manipulated paper and carbons, cursed, lit a cigarette and started to type.

Inspector Ware put his head round the door. 'Oh, there you are, Doug! The old man's on his way and he wants a word before you push off home.'

Kersey had a considerable respect for Detective Chief Superintendent Wycliffe, the boss of CID. But it was based on hearsay, he had never worked with the chief though he admitted that he would have liked the chance. He had almost completed his report when Wycliffe came in. The chief superintendent had an unassuming presence, he was of medium height, slim, with a severe cast of countenance – monkish, in fact. For some time after his appointment he had been known as 'The Monk' but the nickname had been forgotten and he had become like a long line of predecessors, 'the old man'.

Wycliffe pulled up a chair to Kersey's desk, lit his pipe and settled down as though he had all the time in the world. 'In a hurry, Sergeant?'

'Not really, sir. Just the paper-work to finish, then I'm through.'

Wycliffe's manner was relaxed and conversational. 'You never know where you are when a young girl goes missing. You can involve half the force, run up hundreds of hours overtime, cost the tax-payer thousands, neglect everything else and then find that the little devil has just gone off to get herself noticed.'

Kersey nodded. 'But that's better than finding her body under a bush on the common.'

Wycliffe was involved in relighting his pipe but he glanced shrewdly at the sergeant. 'I agree; unfortunately, deploying an army doesn't stop that.'

They chatted about the case for twenty minutes, by which time Wycliffe knew what would be in Kersey's report without having to read it and he had, as a bonus, the benefit of Kersey's asides, his vivid thumb-nail sketches of the inhabitants of Paul's Court and a few Kerseyisms on life in general.

By the same token, Kersey had tentatively sized up his chief. He saw a man with a clear view of right and wrong who was not a bigot; he recognized a close-grained moral toughness with a hint of old-fashioned puritan zeal, but no sign of any wish to burn heretics. A man of compassion but no sentimentalist, a reformer but not a do-gooder.

Both men were well pleased. Wycliffe sat back in his chair. 'All right, what does it amount to?'

Kersey scratched a bristly chin. 'It seems to me that there are three possibilities. First, the girl could have cleared out on her own – angry, disgusted, jealous – she might be any or all of these depending on her temperament – because her mother went to bed with her boyfriend. Second, it's possible that she's gone off, again voluntarily, with some boy or man we haven't heard of yet. Third, some nutter has got hold of her, in which case she's almost certainly dead.'

Wycliffe nodded. 'But if she's gone off voluntarily, isn't it odd that she didn't take her clothes? Then there's the money; surely ninety pounds would have been useful.'

Kersey grimaced. 'As far as the clothes are concerned she might have left them deliberately to worry her mother more. You'd be surprised how spiteful some of these girls can be to their mums. But the money is more of a problem, her mother didn't even know she had it and it would be very interesting to know where she got it.'

Wycliffe tilted his chair at an alarming angle. 'One thing we must do is to find out whether anybody else is missing from among her acquaintances. The diary might help there. Can't her mother identify any of the initials?'

'Seems not.'

'Then I'll get somebody on to it. Now about your third possibility – the nutter theme?'

'That's where the big battalions come in. Saturation coverage, and even then you need more than average copper's luck.'

Wycliffe brought his chair back on an even keel. 'I think I've got the picture. In the morning, if she still hasn't turned up, we'll lay on a limited operation. Inspector Ware has already checked with the hospitals and circulated her description so I shall put a few chaps on visiting coffee bars and discos, checking with bus crews and at stations. I want you to carry on with the girl's background and contacts.'

'You want me to stay on the case, sir?' Kersey was surprised.

'Of course. As investigating officer you must be in whatever team there is.'

Kersey watched the superintendent leave and reflected that this was one of few encounters with top brass when he did not feel that he had been scarred in battle. He grinned to himself. 'Perhaps we're both on the same side.'

Kersey arrived home at his semi-detached in the early darkness. People along the road were returning from their excursions, unpacking picnic gear and children, carrying tired, whimpering toddlers indoors to bath and bed.

'Have you had a meal?'

Kersey's wife, Esther, believed that the greatest risk to any policeman comes, not from a well directed brick, bottle or even bullet, but from unsuitable meals eaten at unsuitable times.

'I've got some cold meat and I can do you a salad.'

'Where are the girls?'

'Over at Kathy's.'

When he had finished in the bathroom he pushed open the door of the girls' room. Books overflowed everywhere, there were aquarium tanks containing God knows what, a cheap microscope, a record player, records not in their sleeves, clothes on the floor and all manner of prints and pictures stuck to the walls. A sight which usually dismayed him but tonight he looked at it with approval.

Toby Pongo Lennon arrived late for his ginger cake. It was evening and the Hedleys had settled down to their nightly routine; the old lady seated at the piano while her husband paced round the house a cigarette dangling from his lips. If it had not been for one of his periodic visits to the verandah it is unlikely that Toby would have made himself heard.

'Hullo, my boy, it's you! Your aunt said you would be here and she's right for once.'

Toby behaved like a dutiful nephew, thoughtfully deferential. 'How is aunt? I'm afraid it's a long time since I've been over, but you know how it is . . . '

The sound of the piano ceased abruptly and Mrs Hedley's bitonal bleat came from the living-room. 'Who is it? Who have you got out there? Is that you, Toby?'

'Yes, it's me, aunt Emmie; come to see you at last.' He

went through to the living-room and kissed his aunt. 'Things don't change here – just the same as when I was home.'

'It's where you should be now, my boy,' his aunt said, 'But we won't talk about that. I knew you would come; I said so to your uncle but, as usual, he didn't believe me. I even baked one of your ginger cakes.' She got up. 'I'll make some coffee.'

Hedley waited for his wife to disappear into the kitchen: 'If it isn't the piano it's the radio and it goes on from morning to night; I get classical music running out of my ears.'

'You're looking well, uncle.'

'Oh, I keep pretty well; pretty well. What are you doing with yourself? Got a job?'

Lennon sat down. 'Not exactly a regular job, uncle, but a bit here and a bit there; I manage.'

'Still living with the Goppel boy?'

'Freddie is still sharing with me, yes.'

'You should find yourself a nice girl. I don't like this business of two cockerels sharing the same roost.'

'Ask him if he's heard the news,' Mrs Hedley called from the kitchen.

'News, aunt?'

Hedley said, 'She means about the Cole girl – you remember the Coles.'

'You mean Natalie.'

'Not Natalie, her daughter – she's disappeared.'

'But she's only a kid.'

'She's fifteen, old enough to meet and make trouble these days. Anyway, we've had the police here questioning everybody.'

'What do they think has happened to her?'

Hedley shook his head. 'God knows what they think; I suppose she's gone off with some man.'

Mrs Hedley came in with a tray. 'Now you just tuck in

73

to that, Toby. I'm sure you don't feed yourself properly. I expected you earlier.'

Lennon said, 'Did you, aunt? As a matter of fact I would have been here earlier but I had a late night and I stopped in bed until lunchtime.'

'Late night?'

'Oh, just a party – a chap who lives in Grenville Road. You may remember me speaking of Jeremy Hobson; he was at school with me. He's married now and he lives in Grenville Road.'

Hedley said, 'Only the upper crust can afford Grenville Road.'

Lennon nodded. 'I'll say! But the Hobsons have pots of money. Jeremy is on the boards of several companies already. That was it, really – a chance to make contacts. As you know, uncle, you can't get far without contacts these days.'

An hour later, when he was leaving, his aunt slipped three crisp notes into his hand.

CHAPTER FOUR

The Wards' Taxi rounded the corner into Falcon Street. Half-past six and already the sun was shining but Alison had had little sleep on the train and she felt chilled and empty inside. For the twentieth time her mother hoped that Henry had managed all right on his own.

'I do hope he had proper meals.'

Alison said, 'If he ate half you left for him he won't be able to move for a month.'

Her father was looking at the taximeter and searching in his pockets for change. 'I'll bet he's still in bed, fast asleep.'

'Are you very tired, dear?'

'Not really, mum.'

'You don't *have* to go to school, one day isn't going to make all that difference.'

'I'd rather go.'

Remarkably, Henry was at the side-door to receive them. Alison thought he looked a bit wan and her mother fussed over him but it was only when they were upstairs with their baggage that he told them.

'You'll have to know sometime, Yvette is missing.'

'*Missing*?'

'Her mother hasn't seen her since Saturday lunch-time. The police are looking for her.'

'The police!'

Alison's father said, 'I suppose they're bound to take it pretty seriously when a young girl goes missing.'

'But they don't think anything has happened to her, surely?'

The novelty of arriving home in the early hours was gone, they were suddenly very tired and deflated.

Henry said, 'There's coffee made and there are eggs in the saucepan . . .'

They drank their coffee but nobody felt like eating and as Henry was persuaded to tell the full story Mrs Ward became increasingly apprehensive. 'You mean the police actually questioned you?'

'Of course.'

'But why? What could you possibly know?'

And so it went on until at half-past seven Kersey arrived. He was very polite and apologized for troubling them so early. 'Really it was Alison I wanted to see. How well did you know Yvette, Alison?'

Alison hesitated and Mrs Ward said, 'They weren't friends—'

'It's best to let Alison speak for herself.' Kind but firm.

'We both caught the same bus to school from the end of the street and sometimes we came back together in the evening so I suppose we saw each other quite often.'

'But as your mother said, you weren't friends – you didn't go out together at weekends, for instance?'

'No.'

'What sort of things did she talk about? Did she tell you about her family or friends? Did she ever mention her father?'

'Well, no . . .'

'As far as you know, has she got many friends?'

It lasted about ten minutes then Kersey began to talk to Alison's parents, skilfully drawing them out about the people in the Court. Mr Ward left the talking to his wife.

According to Mrs Ward they were all nice people; from Willy Goppel, who was really like an uncle to the children, to Geoff Bishop who, whatever people said about him, had always been a gentleman to her. She was sorry for Joan Fiske and for Marty who was a charming and gentle boy. Mr Fiske could sometimes be a bit overbearing but he had business worries. 'It's no joke running any sort of business in these days.' As for the Hedleys, Mrs Ward made them sound like the original Darby and Joan. 'He was an official with the council but he retired at sixty – made redundant when they re-organized his department. Of course he got his pension but he continued to work – several jobs, but finally he went to work in Mr Fiske's office and he only finished there a year back . . . '

Alison and Henry got ready for school which shocked their mother. 'Surely you ought to show some respect . . . '

'Best to let them carry on as usual,' Kersey said. 'We don't know that anything serious has happened to Yvette.'

Alison went off to school with her head in a whirl; she had been less than frank with the policeman, not that she had anything to hide but because what she might have said would have discredited Yvette without doing anybody any good. 'It's not as though I *believed* it,' Alison told herself. 'She made it up to impress me.'

For some reason Yvette had always seemed anxious to impress and, perhaps, shock her. On more than one occasion while they were walking down the street to the bus stop or standing waiting she had treated Alison to alleged revelations about her sex life.'

'Have you ever slept with a man?'

'No.'

'You mean that you're still a virgin?'

'Yes.'

'Good God!' And she had looked at Alison as though she were some strange creature from another world. 'I started two years ago.'

77

'But you were only thirteen!' Alison had not meant to give her encouragement but the words seemed to have been forced from her.

Yvette was complacent. 'I know. It was Geoff Bishop, when he first came to live with my mother. Of course I was a bit simple then and I told mother and she raised hell. But afterwards I got to thinking, "Well, if that's what they want . . ." So now I make them pay.'

'You mean you take money?'

'Of course! What do I get out of it otherwise? There's nothing in it for the woman. It's just dead boring.'

Alison had thought about this and similar talks many times. It could *not* be true. But if it was . . . She was very troubled in her mind.

On his way to police headquarters that morning Wycliffe made a detour to take in Falcon Street. He had never allowed himself to become desk-bound but he sometimes almost regretted the promotion which had taken him 'off the ground'. There was nowhere to park in Falcon Street so he left his car in parallel Church Street and walked through Church Lane with the wall of the churchyard on one side and Paul's Court on the other. He noticed the little iron gate giving pedestrian access to the lane from the Court.

It was half-past eight and Falcon Street was coming alive; the butcher down the street was at work with cleaver and saw, the delicatessen opened its doors as he arrived, and sales girls were waiting outside the mini-market for the manager to unlock. He could not have explained why he had to see all this but he knew that otherwise the people Kersey had described would never be real to him – Natalie Cole, Geoff Bishop, Henry and the Wards, the Fiskes, the Hedleys and Willy Goppel.

A fair girl carrying a briefcase came out of the Court

and set off up the street. That must be Alison. She was followed a minute or two later by a sandy-haired lad on a moped, presumably her brother. Outside the wine-shop a window cleaner started work with bucket and mop. A man, well-dressed and self-important, carrying a briefcase, came through the archway and turned up the street in the direction of the bus-stop. Martin Fiske? One would have expected him to be driving unless he was a keep-fit addict. Bishop – unmistakable – followed a few minutes later, pumping the accelerator pedal of a souped-up Cortina. It was going to be another fine day and the sun was already gaining strength. Wycliffe stood under the pillared portico of the Old Mansion House, now used as offices by a firm of solicitors and an estate agent. He walked as far as Willy Goppel's shop and peered through the glass. The frontage was narrow and the little shop was full of dolls' houses stacked one on top of the other and there was a great variety of miniature furniture displayed on the dusty shelves.

On the stroke of nine the doors of the post office opened and, to Wycliffe's surprise, Kersey came out, seen off by a tall, thin, harassed looking man of middle age. Kersey did not appear in the least surprised to see Wycliffe.

'Morning, sir. I've been having a chat with the Wards, they came back round six this morning. Of course the boy told them what had happened.'

'I think I saw the girl and her brother leaving for school.'

Kersey nodded. 'I got here early to have a word with the girl in particular. She seems a nice kid, sensible and not bitchy. According to her Yvette is a pretty average sort of girl – not academic and thoroughly fed-up with school, but by no means a young tart. Not the sort to do anything really daft.'

Kersey glanced at Willy Goppel's shop. 'I asked Ward

about Goppel and he said he does occasionally go away at the weekends but he's usually back by mid-morning on Monday.'

'Any idea where he goes?'

'Ward doesn't know. He says Goppel is a nice chap but doesn't talk much about himself. He owns a lot of property.' Kersey went on to tell Wycliffe about the incident over Goppel's papers which he had sent to the Home Office. 'I expect you saw it in the reports, sir.'

'If I did, I don't remember it.'

'Well, the theft was several weeks ago, but that wasn't important. The papers came to us only on Thursday, and that was when I talked to Goppel.'

After seeing Martin Fiske leave for work Mrs Hedley allowed a decent interval to elapse before crossing the Court to call on Joan Fiske whom she found in the middle of vacuuming the living-room.

'Never mind, Emmie, it doesn't matter, I can do this any time . . . Could you do with a cup of coffee or is it too early?'

Since the initial breaking of the ice Joan Fiske had been twice more to consult Mrs Hedley but this was the first time the Mountain had come to Mahomet. It seemed that they were becoming friends and already they were on first-name terms.

'Odd, when you come to think of it, after living next door to each other all these years . . . '

Both women went into the kitchen where they could chat while the coffee was brewing.

'They've still not found her.'

Joan Fiske said, 'The police seem to be making a lot of fuss. I mean, the most likely thing is that she's gone off with some boy. She's a real young madam, going around with "Restricted Area" printed across her bosom. In my day she'd have been arrested.'

Mrs Hedley nodded. 'I blame her mother. All the same I can't help feeling that something has happened to the child.'

'You mean . . . ?'

'I've got that *feeling* and I'm seldom wrong.'

Joan Fiske was intrigued. 'I suppose there's no way of finding out what the cards have to say?'

'Of course. You can do a Reading for anybody, they don't have to be present, though it helps.'

'You mean you could do a Reading for the girl?'

Mrs Hedley shook her head. 'No, I draw the line at that, I've never Read for minors but I could do one for her mother.'

'*Really?* You wouldn't care to . . . '

'I'll get the cards.' It was astonishing how much more sprightly Mrs Hedley seemed to become whenever there was something going on which interested her.

By the time she returned Joan Fiske had the living-room habitable and a small table with two chairs placed in a good light. The old lady had not forgotten her black silk square which she placed in the middle of the table.

'I suppose you've no idea when her birthday is?'

'I do, as it happens, I remember when she took out some sort of policy with Martin he said that it was the same as his – that's April the third.'

'So she's Aries, which means the Significator should come from the suit of Clubs. She would chose the Knight.'

'How on earth do you know that?'

'The old lady smiled. 'Never mind. You shuffle for her.'

The cards were laid out and Mrs Hedley meditated on them while Joan Fiske maintained a respectful silence. On more than one occasion Mrs Hedley started to speak then changed her mind. In the end she said, 'I don't like the look of this. If it was anyone else but you I would refuse to Read.'

Joan Fiske said, 'Surely it can't do any harm?'

The old lady pursed her lips. 'No, the harm has already been done. Look at the three cards of the Major Arcana – all reversed, the Empress, Temperance, and Force. You could scarcely have a clearer picture of the woman. Sensuality, an unstable temperament, a complete disregard for others and the implication that self-indulgence – *physical* self-indulgence could cost her dear, perhaps *someone who means much to her*.'

Mrs Hedley turned her grey eyes on her disciple to emphasize the point. There was a long interval during which the old lady continued to brood over the Tarot. At one point a fly alighted on her nose and she seemed totally unaware of it.

Joan Fiske ventured, 'What about the other lines?'

It was as though Mrs Hedley had gone into some sort of trance for she turned from the cards with a blank look in her eyes. 'What?'

'The other lines.'

'Oh, it's the same story. I've never come across a first Reading like it. Look! The two of Cups reversed, the Knave of Swords and the five of Money – sex again, and jealousy this time – and greed. But a dark, secretive child is involved as a source of bad news. *A dark secretive child – a source of bad news* . . .' Mrs Hedley stared at her companion with disturbing intensity.

'But that doesn't necessarily mean that Yvette . . .'

The old lady shook her head. 'No, it doesn't but look at this in the next line. It begins with the nine of Swords – danger, a serious illness, or *news of a death* . . .'

Suddenly she swept the cards into a heap. 'I don't want to go on with this!' She remained motionless for a full minute, her long, bony fingers spread over the jumbled cards, then she turned with a twisted smile which was half apologetic, 'Sometimes the cards get the better of me.'

Joan Fiske was impressed. 'It's astonishing! I would never have believed it if I hadn't seen it with my own eyes.'

Wycliffe and Kersey were still on the pavement outside the Dolls' House shop. Wycliffe said, 'I shall be at headquarters all day, keep in touch and let me know when Goppel gets back.'

Kersey was surprised by the importance which Wycliffe seemed to attach to the toy-maker. He glanced at his watch, 'Well, he shouldn't be long, it's ten o'clock already.'

Wycliffe was on the point of turning up Church Lane when there was a shout and a man in overalls came running along the pavement towards them. 'You're the police, aren't you?'

The man was middle-aged, flushed and breathless. 'I've found the girl . . . She's lying between my shed and the wall . . . She's half naked and she's dead.'

Kersey took him by the arm and walked him back to the entrance of the churchyard. 'Who are you?'

'Me? I'm the sexton. My name's Couch – Jim Couch.' He wiped his forehead with the back of his hand. 'Christ, I had a shock when I saw her! I look after the church and the graveyard and I dump all my grass cuttings, prunings and so forth on a heap between my shed and the wall. I went there with a barrow-load and there she was . . . '

There was a little brick-built toolshed with a space of four or five feet between it and the wall of the church-yard adjacent to Church Lane. Yvette's slight, pale body was lying sprawled on a mound of rubbish. She wore her jeans but she was naked to the waist. She had been strangled.

There was no point in disturbing the body.

Within half-an-hour the churchyard was over-run by

police and their ancillaries; a large area was being roped off and a canvas screen erected. There were uniformed men at the gates and a van was on its way with a temporary coffin. Sergeant Smith, photographer to Wycliffe's squad, arrived and started taking photographs, first of the body, then of the immediate neighbourhood. Detectives were going over the ground looking for whatever they could find. Dr Franks, the pathologist, was expected at any moment.

Detective Inspector Scales was in charge and Wycliffe told him to ask the vicar to allow the use of the church hall as an incident post until an incident-van arrived.

Church Lane was closed and a small crowd began to collect in Falcon Street though they were constantly moved on.

It was fairly obvious that Yvette's body had been pushed over the wall and it interested Wycliffe to see that this had been done at a point immediately opposite the little iron gate which led into Paul's Court.

'It looks as though we may have to look very near home.'

Kersey nodded.

'We'd better tell the mother, there are enough people here.'

Natalie came to the door wearing a housecoat and looking as though she had not slept. 'Ah, it's you. Any . . .?' She broke off. 'I can see from your faces, you don't have to tell me, she's dead.'

They followed her into the living-room where she poured herself a whisky. 'What about you?'

'Not now.'

'Where was she found?'

'In the churchyard.'

'Had she been . . . '

'It doesn't look like it.'

'How did she die?'

84

'She was strangled.'

There was no point in mincing words with Natalie, all her life she had rubbed shoulders with violence.

'Poor little devil! When can I see her?'

'I'll take you along in about an hour.'

She nodded. 'I'd better get dressed.'

'Are you all right?'

'I'm not going to faint or cut my throat if that's what you mean.'

'We'll be back.'

Out in the courtyard Marty was walking round and round the oak tree.

Wycliffe glanced at his watch. 'It's gone eleven, you'd better see if your friend Goppel is back yet.'

'You think he might have killed the kid and scarpered?'

'No, but it's a possibility.'

Kersey left Wycliffe standing under the tree. Marty stopped his orbiting and looked at him, ' 'vette gone?'

'Yes, Marty.'

'Gone away?'

'Yes.'

Marty nodded his head slowly. He made a curious gesture with his hands as though trying to communicate something then, finding the effort too great, gave up.

Kersey came back. 'Nobody home.'

They walked back to the churchyard where things were quietening down. Yvette's body had been removed. Franks, the baby-faced pathologist, was on the point of leaving. Wycliffe and he had worked together so often that there was no ceremony between them.

'What did you make of her?'

Franks shrugged. 'I'll tell you more this afternoon but I'd guess that she's been dead for more than twenty-four hours. The scratches on her arms and breasts are almost certainly postmortem injuries –

85

probably caused by the twigs of the bushes and the stonework of the wall.'

Franks ran his hand through thinning sandy hair. 'Odd case, isn't it? I mean, what was the motive? It's unlikely that she's been raped. Some weirdo, that's for sure. A bosom fetish or something. It takes all sorts.'

Franks himself was a notorious philanderer; at fifty plus he was still notching up conquests at a rate which kept him in the Casanova class. 'Can't understand deviants myself; it's as though you could improve on nature.'

Wycliffe, who had had a puritanical upbringing, disapproved of this kind of talk. 'Yes, well, let me know as soon as you can. I've arranged for her mother to see her at about noon. Is that all right?'

'That should be okay. See you!' Franks went to his parked car which looked more like a weapon than a means of transport, the engine roared out decibels and he was gone.

'He must be trying hard to prove something to somebody,' Kersey said.

Inspector Scales had established a temporary base in the church hall and he came over to Wycliffe. 'Her bag was under her body.'

There it was on one of the tables, the contents spread out beside it. They included a purse, lipstick, handkerchief, a key, a sachet of aspirin tablets, a small bag of sweets and a medicine bottle full of some clear liquid bearing a chemist's label with Saturday's date. There was also a dog-eared piece of paper on which somebody had written a prescription.

'Camphor, aether, aspirin, liquor ammoniæ, benzoic acid, oil of anise . . . Some sort of 'flu mixture?'

Scales nodded. 'That's what I thought but we can check with the chemist.'

The purse contained a five-pound note, four singles and some loose change.

At a little before mid-day Wycliffe picked Natalie up in his new Granada. She was wearing her blue dress with white facings and she carried a matching handbag. She wore little make-up and anyone might have taken her for an ordinary suburban housewife . . . '

Wycliffe drove through the city centre and out on the other side of town. The mortuary was attached to the pathology department of the city hospital. They waited in a bare little room like a doctor's waiting room and after five minutes they were fetched by a white-coated attendant.

Yvette's body lay on a trolley covered by a sheet. At a sign from Wycliffe the attendant lifted the edge of the sheet, exposing the slightly discoloured features of the dead girl. Natalie stared at the face briefly then, taking the edge of the sheet, she whisked it clear, uncovering the naked body. The attendant looked scandalized.

'Is this how she was found?'

'No, she was wearing her jeans, socks and sandals; they have been sent to forensic.'

'What about the scratches?'

'She was scratched by the bushes.'

The attendant looked from one to the other in astonishment at this calm exchange. He moved to replace the sheet but she stopped him with a gesture and pointed to the girl's hand nearest her. 'Why have they cut her nails?'

Wycliffe looked at the attendant who shook his head.

'She must have cut them herself.'

Natalie turned to him with a curious expression which had in it a certain pride. 'Like that? Never! Yvette was proud of her nails; she wasn't fussy about the rest of her appearance but she never neglected her nails. She had nice hands and she knew it.'

The attendant replaced the sheet.

Natalie said, 'Do you want me any more?'

'Just a couple of questions and your signature on a form.'

She followed Wycliffe into the waiting-room. 'Well?'

'Her handbag was found near her and apart from the usual things there was a full bottle of medicine – influenza mixture. I wondered if you had any idea who it was for?'

'Not for her, anyway. She would never take any medicine apart from the occasional aspirin.'

'So you can't help us there. The other question concerned any trinkets or jewellery she might have been wearing – necklace, rings, bracelets?'

'Only her watch, she always wore that.'

'What sort of watch?'

'Just an ordinary wrist watch, nothing expensive. It had a bracelet made up of lucky charms – you know the sort of thing.'

Natalie signed the form which the clerk had prepared for her.

'Now, I'll take you home.'

'No, drop me off at La Cass, it's better to be working.'

Wycliffe dropped her outside the club. In all the ordeal not a single tear, not a word of sentiment, just a hint of pride when she mentioned the girl's nails. And yet Wycliffe felt sure that Natalie was grieving, silently and without demonstration, as an animal grieves.

Back in Falcon Street they had succeeded in man-oeuvring one of the big blue incident-vans through the gates of the churchyard to be parked on the gravel. These vans offered limited office accommodation and provided radio and telephone links.

As Wycliffe got out of his car he was accosted by two

reporters, the first of many. 'Nothing to say at the moment, you know as much as I do.'

Inspector Scales was already installed in the van and he was on the telephone to the chemist whose label appeared on Yvette's bottle of medicine.

'Mr Martin? ... I'm enquiring about a bottle of medicine – influenza mixture, I think it is – dispensed by you sometime on Saturday ... No, there's nothing wrong with it as far as I know, we merely want to know when it was dispensed and who for . . . '

The conversation continued for a while then Scales replaced the receiver.

'He says the prescription was brought in by a young girl on Saturday evening and that she waited for it to be made up. She told him that it was for somebody with 'flu. Apparently quite a few people have their own prescriptions for their ailments and insist on them being made up even when there is an identical proprietary medicine available off the shelf.'

'Did he say what time she was in his shop?'

'At about half-past five.'

Another piece in the jigsaw of Yvette's movements on Saturday afternoon and evening.

'Is Kersey about?'

'No, I think he's taking his meal break but he shouldn't be long. Incidentally, Willy Goppel hasn't turned up yet.'

It was odd about Goppel.

The police had finished their main task in the churchyard but three men were engaged in a systematic search for anything which might have been missed and they were joined by a couple of press photographers. A TV van was cruising down Falcon Street, looking for somewhere to park.

Scales said, 'I hope this isn't going to be one of those.'

Wycliffe knew what he meant. A couple of potentially

sensational cases will pass by scarcely noticed by the press then, for no apparent reason, one hits the head-lines and stays there throughout the investigation with almost as many pressmen as policemen on the ground.

Wycliffe tried to focus his ideas. Yvette might have been attacked in Church Lane or even in the churchyard but it seemed at least as likely that she had been killed in a nearby house. No prizes for guessing which. Her mother would have arrived home at about three when Yvette had been alone in the house with Bishop for several hours . . .

A quick and easy solution? After all, murder is more often than not a domestic crime.

When Kersey returned from his meal break Wycliffe aired his thoughts and the sergeant agreed. He was sent to talk to Bishop.

Fenton Street was as different from Falcon Street as two streets can be. A quite unnecessarily wide road cut through a random assortment of dreary concrete block-houses with an occasional gap where a starved and anaemic tree struggled half-heartedly for survival – the planners' concession to 'the environment'. Bishop's Car Mart and Vehicle Hire Service had a forecourt full of old bangers and a huge, asbestos-roofed shed with a con-crete façade painted a bilious shade of green and lettered in red.

Kersey and his colleagues had been taking an interest in Bishop for more than a year – since each of three break-ins on the industrial estate had employed one of his hired vans, later to be found abandoned on the motorway.

'You can't expect me to know whether a client who hires a van is a crook, Mr Kersey. I mean, once I'm satisfied that he has a licence to drive the class of vehicle concerned and he's paid his deposit . . . '

There was also some question about insurance write-offs turning up in new and beguiling fancy dress.

Kersey made his way among the hardware to the office which consisted of two rooms, one for the receptionist and an inner one for Bishop. The receptionist was nowhere to be seen and Kersey went through. Bishop was seated at a roll-topped desk tapping his teeth with a ball-point while he studied a battered loose-leaf ledger. He swivelled round in his chair.

'Mr Kersey! Have a pew. Evelyn's gone to spend a penny.'

Kersey continued to stand. 'I suppose you've heard about Yvette?'

Bishop registered grave concern. 'I have. Natalie rang me; she's pretty cut up, poor girl. Well, it's natural, isn't it? I mean, I feel pretty rough about it myself. I know I'm not her father but I've lived in the same house for some time now. She was a good kid.'

Kersey found himself staring at a calendar picture of a nude girl who by suitable contortion had contrived to get her breasts and buttocks in the same picture and still look pleased about it.

'When did you last see Yvette?'

Bishop fiddled with the ends of his bandit moustache. 'I suppose I saw her some time on Saturday but I can't remember for sure. I mean, you don't take much notice of somebody living in the same house.'

Purely as a matter of tactics Kersey stared at him as though in disbelief and it worked; Bishop put his pen on the desk with great deliberation. 'You're quite right, Mr Kersey, Yvette looked in here to see me on Saturday afternoon. It had gone out of my mind.'

'What time?'

'Time?' He screwed up his features. 'Fourish? A bit later, perhaps. I can't say exactly.'

'What did she want?'

'Oh, she often looks in here when she's passing.'

'What did she want?'

91

Bishop shrugged: 'If you must know she wanted a part-time job. We open seven days a week and she wanted to work here Saturdays and Sundays.'

'Did you agree?'

'No. For two reasons. First, Natalie wouldn't have gone for it and second, I haven't much use for a girl about the place weekends. I mean it's when the chaps come to buy cars and a girl of fifteen can't be expected to flog bangers.' Bishop tried hard to look and sound reasonable.

'Why did she want the job?'

'Why do any of us? You know how it is with youngsters these days, Mr Kersey; where we used to think in terms of a few bob they think in fivers.'

'What did you say to her?'

'Well, what could I say? I told her it was no dice.'

'How did she take it?'

'She was disappointed but I chatted her up a bit and when she left she was laughing. After all, I'm the only one who can talk to her something like a father.'

Kersey looked at him solemnly. 'You should take up social work; you're wasted flogging bangers to mugs.' He lit a cigarette and settled in his chair. 'Did you ever give her money?'

'Money? No, Natalie wouldn't have stood for it.'

Bishop sat waiting for more questions and when none came he began to fidget. 'If that's all you want to ask me, Mr Kersey . . . '

'What time did you get home Saturday night?'

The question took him momentarily off balance. 'Saturday? Oh, it must have been half-eleven or thereabouts.'

'Was Yvette home?'

Bishop glowered. 'I don't like that, Mr Kersey, you know bloody well she wasn't. Of course, I didn't know it at the time, I thought she'd be in bed as usual.'

'Where did you spend Saturday evening?'

'Actually, in the local boozer with a few of the lads –
The Sportsman's in Falcon Street.'

'So you didn't take your car.'

'No, I walked.'

'Did you notice anything unusual on your way home
– hear anything, see anything?'

'Bishop shook his head. 'No, I didn't. Nothing;
between you and me I was pretty far gone.'

Naturally the Wards at the post office had heard the
news almost at once, now customers stood about the
shop, mostly in silence but occasionally exchanging a
few words in low voices as if in church. Falcon Street
was old-fashioned enough to mourn its dead.

Mr Hedley was sent to buy stamps and to find out
what had happened. When he returned his wife was in
the kitchen preparing their mid-day meal.

'Well?'

'They've found her.'

'Alive?'

'No, the sexton, Jim Couch, found her; she was lying
on a pile of rubbish behind his shed, strangled.'

Mrs Hedley softened, 'Poor child.'

Hedley sighed. 'Apparently the body was pushed
over the wall.'

Mrs Hedley left her preparations for the meal and
went across to tell Joan Fiske who looked at her with
something approaching awe.

'You *knew*!'

The old lady shook her head. 'No, I merely *felt*, but
the cards knew.' After a moment she went on, 'Her
body was pushed over the wall right opposite the gate
from our Court.'

Mrs Fiske clasped her hands. 'Oh, my God! You mean
that it was somebody from the Court!'

Mrs Hedley looked round as though she feared being

93

overheard and lowered her voice. 'I'll tell you something but I don't want it repeated; you understand?'

'Of course.'

'It's something my husband said he saw. You know he goes out on our verandah at all times of the day and night – he's old and he gets restless . . . '

'Yes, I often see him there.'

'Well, he was out there late on Saturday night and he says he saw somebody behaving very strangely – very strangely indeed. He said he thought this person came out of Willy Goppel's but he might equally have come through the gate.'

'But who . . . ?'

The old lady shook her head. 'I'm saying no more! You'll have to work it out for yourself. But just think – who in this Court would be likely to assault a fifteen-year-old girl? And who would have the best chance with this particular girl?'

'But shouldn't Mr Hedley tell the police?'

'No! That's what he wants to do, but do you think they would take any notice of an old man? And if they did, could they act on it? It is not as though he saw this man doing anything actually incriminating. And what would happen if this person got to hear that we were making accusations? I wouldn't feel safe in my bed – two old people living alone.'

Joan Fiske was scared herself, 'Yes, I hadn't thought. Of course, if Mr Hedley hasn't got any actual evidence . . . ' She shivered. 'Really, I wish you hadn't told me; I'm nervous enough as it is.'

To Marty it seemed a very long time since he had seen Mr Goppy's cat and he felt uneasy. Any interruption in the even tenor of his life disturbed him and made him feel vaguely restless and unhappy. Several times that morning he had leaned on the rail of Mr Goppy's yard and called softly, 'Fritzy! Fritzy!' But nothing had happened. Now that he had had his lunch he tried again. 'Fritzy!' But the cat did not come and he did not hear the familiar, tentative little cry with which Fritzy sometimes greeted him. He became increasingly concerned and it occurred to him that he had not seen Mr Goppy for a long time either. Perhaps they had gone away together – gone away like Yvette . . . He did not like it when people went away.

Greatly daring he raised the latch of Mr Goppy's gate and entered the yard. He looked back anxiously to make sure that he was unobserved and then advanced to peer through the glass panel of Mr Goppy's back door. He could not see anything very clearly but he thought there was somebody inside moving, then he realized that he was seeing his own reflection in the glass. It amused him and he tried several exaggerated movements which made him chuckle. But he did not forget the cat. Once or twice in the past he had crept into the workshop very quietly when Mr Goppy was at work on his little house and Mr Goppy had not been in the least angry. He would stand watching until he became bored and then say politely, 'I got to go now, Mr Goppy.'

Very gently he turned the door-knob and to his surprise the door opened. He knew that if Mr Goppy was away it should have been locked so he felt relieved. He called again in a voice scarcely above a whisper, 'Fritzy!' But the only response came from the animals in their cages, scuffling and scratching and squeaking. He had forgotten about them and for a moment he was frightened, then he remembered and went over to look at them. He stood for some time by the cages, his hands caressing the wire mesh. He liked the guinea-pigs but he was a little afraid of the lizards so he tried not to see them or only looked at them out of the corner of his eye.

A slight creaking noise startled him and he called out, 'Mr Goppy!' But no-one answered and after a little while he plucked up courage and worked his way round the central bench to the door at the far end of the workshop where he had never been before. With great boldness he opened the door and found himself in a little room at the bottom of a flight of stairs, but what interested him was yet another glass door through which he could see into the shop. He was delighted to be able to look through to the street and see the cars going by, but then came another of those disturbing creaks and it seemed much closer. He looked up the stairs and at first he could not make out what it was he saw, something was hanging over the stairs, swinging very gently; it seemed large and shapeless in the dim light and he was intrigued. At the same time he realized that it was this swinging object which made the occasional creaking noise and he felt reassured. Then, abruptly, as though his eyes had come suddenly into sharp focus, he saw what it was, it was Mr Goppy. Mr Goppy with a blue string round his neck, hanging like a balloon. Marty stood for a long time, wide-eyed, fascinated, then all at once he was overcome by a nameless terror and he fled. He blundered through the workshop and the yard and raced across the Court, up the verandah steps and through the house to the kitchen where his mother was washing dishes.

'What on earth . . . ?'

But Marty was beyond words, he merely tugged at her arm and pointed wildly.

Wycliffe met them by Willy Goppel's little gate, Mrs Fiske, pale and scared, Marty in a state of intense excitement.

'I think something must have happened in there.'

CHAPTER FIVE

Wycliffe looked up the stairwell and saw a man's body suspended by a blue cord from the top landing. He could make out the stockinged feet, dark trousers and light fawn jacket. The body oscillated slowly on the suspending cord as it was disturbed by draughts. He climbed the stairs to the first landing where his face was level with that of the hanging man. Wycliffe was seeing Willy Goppel for the first time and Willy was dead; there was nothing to be done. His features were livid, his lips blue, his eyes bulged slightly and the tip of his tongue protruded from his mouth. The blue, nylon cord was anchored to the newel post of the banisters on the top landing.

He heard a cat crying and opened one of the doors off the landing. A marmalade cat ran out of the room and padded quickly downstairs with one frightened backward glance. Wycliffe returned to the workshop; the key of the back-door was on the inside so he took it, let himself out and locked the door behind him.

At the incident post Scales was on duty and Kersey had just returned from interviewing Bishop.

'Goppel is dead; it looks as though he hanged himself.'

Kersey said, 'So he didn't scarper.'

Scales asked, 'Has this anything to do with the girl?'

'God knows! But we must assume that it has. If she was killed in Goppel's house there might be something to give us a lead and it will be too late to think of that when the whole place has been trampled over.'

Half-an-hour later Willy's house was a scene of ordered chaos with numbers of large men and one woman each intent on a specific task. The one woman was Lucy Crabbe – the first fully operational woman detective to be attached to Wycliffe's squad.

Wycliffe had briefed them before letting them loose. 'You may think this is a lot of fuss about a suicide but it's possible that Yvette Cole was murdered in this house and if she was there is sure to be some evidence of the fact. It's your job to find it, not to trample it out of existence. Don't move round more than you have to, keep to the sides of stairs and corridors and think twice before you touch anything.'

Dr Franks arrived, breezy as ever. 'Business is looking up! What are you calling this? Suicide or murder? I've never come across murder by hanging but I expect it's been done. This will delay my report on the girl. Can't be in two places at once – not on the money they pay me.'

It is impossible to document and record a whole house in the detail necessary to ensure that nothing has been missed. Which surfaces to fingerprint? Which to ignore? From where does one take dust samples and where does one stop taking them? At best it is a hit-and-miss business but after years of experience a good jack develops something of a sixth sense which gives him slightly better odds than chance in getting it right.

Wycliffe remained in the workshop where, presumably, Willy had spent most of his working hours. He marvelled at the dolls' house which might now never be completed. It seemed to be a model of a late Georgian town house with, as far as Wycliffe could judge, every detail represented accurately to scale. In theory he was attracted to model making, he had something of the peep-show mentality, but he knew that in fact he would want a more practical reward for such expenditure of time, skill and patience.

At the end of the workshop, nearest the shop, there were a few shelves with books, and a high desk of the kind once favoured by schoolteachers. The books were all concerned with the architecture of the Georgian, Regency and Victorian periods and, propped against the desk, there was a portfolio of drawings, sketches and plans, evidently Willy's own work.

The desk contained a couple of ledgers in which he kept simple accounts of his dolls' house business; there was a bundle of receipts, a clip of unpaid bills, a few letters from suppliers, cheque book, paying-in book and a folder of bank statements. Flicking through the pages of a desk diary Wycliffe came across a loose sheet of notes written in a careful though spidery hand. It was a list of firms – small firms engaged in retail trade in the city: City Butchers Limited, The Elite Printing and Stationery Company, Excelsior Furnishings Limited . . . About a dozen altogether. Against all but three of the entries was the abbreviated name of an insurance company: Eagle, Sun, Legal, Phoenix . . . with either a tick or a cross. Probably Willy had been trying to get cheaper cover for his properties and had compared notes with other owners.

In addition to all this there were three files of correspondence, one each for Crowther and Grant, solicitors; Cassells and White, estate agents; and The Martin Fiske Business Accountancy Service.

He heard Kersey's voice on the stairs. 'Come up here, sir. Take a look at this . . . '

Wycliffe went upstairs. Willy's body had been removed to a stretcher and was about to be carried downstairs to the waiting mortuary van. Wycliffe followed Kersey into the living-room which was one of the unspoiled rooms of the old house, still with its moulded cornices, ornamental ceiling, carved architraves and marble mantelpiece. Willy's ancient three-piece suite was lost in one corner and most of the rest of the floor space was occupied by trestle tables on which there was a scale model of the whole Court, the houses, the garages, the yards and the gardens – even the oak tree, all convincingly portrayed. But beyond all this there were figures, carved in wood and meticulously painted; they were disposed outside the houses to which they belonged. The Ward family was immediately recognizable; Mr and Mrs Hedley, tall, lean and slightly stooping, brooded over the scene from their verandah; the Fiskes were there with Marty, his head twisted a little on one side in characteristic pose; Natalie, a slim, black-haired siren, was sunbathing – in her bikini. Bishop lounged against the doorpost, unmistakable with his broad shoulders and piratical countenance; and in Yvette Willy had caught the languid posture of bored youth to perfection. Willy's own figure, bent over his sink-gardens, was vaguely defined; enigmatic.

Kersey said, 'This thing is a bit kinky, don't you think? There's something *Alice Through the Looking-Glass* about it, all innocently childish on the surface but underneath, spooky and a bit sinister.' He screwed his face into a grimace, searching for words. 'It's childish all right, but it's the childishness of an adult. When you remember that Willy didn't have to make a living out of dolls' houses and you think of those sink-gardens, then this . . .'

'Go on.'

Kersey was cautious. 'All I'm saying is that it's easy to imagine a man like Willy becoming attracted to young girls – or boys, for that matter. After all, look at Lewis Carroll – or Barrie. Often there's no harm in it but when a lonely man starts fantasising over kids, it's dangerous; there's a risk. Don't you agree?'

'In general, yes. In this case I can't see Yvette as Alice – Lolita, perhaps, but too old for either. However, what

100

you're suggesting is that Goppel murdered the girl and then, in a fit of remorse, hanged himself.'

'It's possible.'

Wycliffe prodded his cheek with the stem of his unlit pipe. 'It's certainly tempting to link Yvette's murder with Goppel's suicide but just imagine for a moment that we didn't have a murder on our hands. Suppose Yvette was still alive and we found Willy like this. With your previous knowledge of his troubles, what would you say?'

'Suicide because of the business with his papers. That would be the reasonable explanation in the circumstances.'

'But Yvette being murdered makes it less so?'

Kersey was dogged. 'I think the two must be linked.'

Wycliffe said, 'You're probably right but we've got to be sure. I want to know who stole Willy's papers and why they were sent to you. There's not much to go on but it seems that whoever did it must have had a grudge against Willy and sufficient acquaintance with the Mallet Street nick to know that you are a D.S. there.'

Kersey grinned. 'And that still leaves it as wide open as a Scotsman's kilt but I'll have a go.'

'Good! By the way, didn't you say Goppel had a son?'

'That's right, he lives with a chap called Toby Lennon – the Hedley's nephew – in Telfer Street, behind the pannier market.'

'He'll have to be told but I'll see to that.'

Willy's living-room was clean but depressingly drab and shabby. He had done his household chores conscientiously but without enthusiasm or much imagination. The old-fashioned fire grate was filled with red crêpe paper for the summer and there was a small electric fire for chilly evenings. The chairs were drawn up, one on each side of the fireplace, and there was an empty whisky glass on the hearth-rug by each chair. A bottle of whisky, half-full, stood in the fender.

'Looks as though he had company,' Wycliffe spoke to Fowler, the detective constable who was searching the living-room.

'Looks like it, sir. With any luck we shall get prints off the glasses.'

Willy Goppel's body was in the van and Franks, the pathologist, came over to Wycliffe.

'Who are you sending?'

A police officer should be present at any post-mortem where there are possible criminal implications.

Wycliffe hesitated. 'I'll send Scales along. I want all the clothing sent to forensic and I want you to look out for scratches and abrasions which might have been caused immediately before death.'

'Why, for God's sake?'

'If he murdered the girl, isn't it likely that she fought back?'

Franks nodded. 'Point taken. Well, if all murderers had the sense to hang themselves it would save the tax-payers a lot of money and put a few lawyers out of work. I'd be all for that.'

Wycliffe was greatly puzzled. He agreed with Kersey that it would be stretching coincidence rather far to suppose that the murder and the suicide were not connected. On the other hand there were difficulties in the theory that Willy had murdered the girl then hanged himself in remorse. Allowing for the fact that lonely, middle-aged men may brood on nubile girls there was little evidence of a sexual motive for the crime. More than that, if Willy had killed her he had gone some way towards covering his tracks – by disposing of the body – before being overwhelmed by guilt.

But in Wycliffe's view the most telling point was a simple one. He had seen the girl and he had seen Willy. In a struggle it was likely that the man might have got the upper hand but not before Yvette had made her mark on him and had time to scream the house down.

Brooding, Wycliffe went upstairs to the top landing where the nylon cord was still secured to the base of the newel post. Sergeant Smith, who doubled as the squad's photographer and finger-print man, was taking flash pictures of everything in sight. He was a middle-aged, dyspeptic misogynist. Wycliffe was tempted to ask him if he had fantasies about teen-aged girls.

'A lot of fuss about a suicide, isn't it, sir?'

Wycliffe muttered something non-committal. It was best to ignore Smith's leading questions.

'A clove-hitch round the newel post,' Smith said, 'and a running noose on the other end. About ten feet of cord altogether.' He stood looking down the stairwell. 'If he went over the banisters he would have had a free fall of eight feet – more than he'd have got from the hangman in the old days. I wonder the jerk didn't dislodge the newel post.'

Wycliffe shook his head. 'He certainly didn't go over from here. His head went into the noose on the landing below.'

Smith looked at him with curiosity. 'How can you know that?'

'You as good as said it yourself. Goppel died of asphyxia – you saw his head and neck. In judicial hanging, with a drop of six feet, death was never due to asphyxia – always to the extension and severance of the spinal cord.'

'You mean that he came up here to fix the rope then went calmly down to the next landing and put his head in the noose, hoisting himself over the banisters – is that it?'

'I've no idea how calm he was but quite apart from the evidence, you know as well as I do that suicides by hanging rarely allow any drop.' As he spoke Wycliffe was looking over the banisters down to the next landing. 'That rail down there doesn't appear to have been dusted for prints.'

'No sir, it hasn't, I didn't think—'

'Then do it now; that's where his head went into the noose. Look for smears as well as prints and for any fibres which might have caught in the joints of the woodwork. Examine the uprights to see if there are any signs of fresh scuffing.'

There were two bedrooms on the top floor, Willy's and another which must have been his son's and was still furnished as a single room. Willy's bedroom could hardly have changed since he shared it with his wife; the furniture was old-fashioned and shabby, the carpet and curtains were faded and whatever pattern there had been on the wallpaper had almost disappeared.

As Wycliffe came into the room D.C. Crabbe was turning over the bedclothes. 'I've just started in here, sir.'

'Don't let me disturb you.'

D.C. Crabbe was an extremely efficient and determined young woman and Wycliffe was sure that she would climb to somewhere near the top or know the reason why. No quarter asked; none given. In her presence it was dangerous even to think of sex.

On the wall over the bed there was a framed photograph of a younger Willy seated next to a thin, frail looking woman with a baby on her lap. Willy had a moustache at that time and he carried more weight; he sat confidently, legs apart, looking at the baby in his wife's arms with a proud smile.

'Was the bed unmade when you came in?'

'No, I disturbed the bedclothes just in case—'

The news that Willy Goppel had hanged himself spread to one or two reporters who lingered in the neighbourhood in the hope of fresh scraps of information on the murder of Yvette, and when Wycliffe arrived back at the incident post others had arrived. Not that suicide by the little German would have had much of a news rating but a possible link with the murder made it a different matter.

'Are you treating this man's death as in any way connected with the murder of Yvette Cole?'

Wycliffe conducted his press conference from the steps of the incident-van.

'We have to consider every possibility but at the moment there is no firm evidence of a connection.'

'Goppel was an elderly bachelor, living alone, spending his time making dolls' houses – don't you think—?'

'Mr Goppel was not a bachelor, he was a widower.'

'All the same, a man in his position might be expected to become sexually frustrated and . . .'

'I am not a psychologist, gentlemen.'

'Do you know yet whether the girl was raped?'

'She was not. There is nothing to suggest that she was sexually assaulted.'

A very little man, wily and persistent, whom Wycliffe knew of old, tried a different line. 'I suppose this will change the nature of your inquiry, superintendent?'

'No, we shall carry on as before.'

'In the expectation of making an arrest?'

'All policemen work in the expectation of an arrest when a crime has been committed.'

'But you can't arrest a dead man.'

'I must admit that I have never tried.'

There was a laugh from the other reporters.

Hedley came in from one of his routine visits to the verandah. 'The police are in Goppel's house. Something must have happened there.'

'What's that?'

Hedley was saved from having to repeat himself by the arrival of Mrs Fiske, so excited that she did not wait for the door to be opened but came in after ringing the bell once.

'Willy Goppel has hanged himself.'

Mrs Hedley looked at her for a moment as though she did not understand, then she said, 'Why? Why did he do that?'

'Well, he must have killed Yvette then hanged himself; they reckon he's been dead since Saturday.'

Mrs Hedley had never seen Joan Fiske so animated, it was almost as though she had been drinking. Mrs Hedley turned to her husband. 'Did you hear that?'

'Of course I heard it but I don't believe it. Willy Goppel wouldn't hurt a fly.'

His wife laughed shortly. 'Not a fly perhaps, but a young girl is a different matter. All men are alike when it comes to sex.'

'But why should he kill her? She used to help him with his animals.'

'Are you purposely stupid? I suppose he tried to rape her and she made a fuss . . . '

Hedley was trying to light a fresh cigarette but his hand trembled. 'I suppose it's possible but I can hardly believe it.'

Mrs Fiske said, 'Oh, it's true all right, I'm so *relieved*.'

The old man looked at her with a gleam of antagonism. 'Why should you be relieved?'

'Because it's all over! It was dreadful having that hanging over us, simply dreadful, and it might have gone on for weeks!'

Mrs Hedley gave Joan Fiske a knowing look. 'Well, at least we can forget about you know who . . . '

Mr Hedley talked but the others took no notice. 'If that's what happened, I suppose it's for the best. If Willy hadn't killed himself they would have put him in prison

106

and he couldn't have stood that. He was like me, he needed his freedom . . . '

Of all the people in the Court Willy's cat adopted the Hedleys and after some preliminary skirmishing Mrs Hedley accepted him.

Telfer Street was narrow and dingy and smitten with planning blight. The blank wall of the market, decorated with spray-painted slogans, formed one side of the street and a row of seedy shops with decaying fronts the other. Most of the rooms over the shops were let as flats and the whole was scheduled for demolition when the spirit moved those in high places and the money-tree bloomed again.

Wycliffe enquired from a little Irishman in a second-hand shop for Goppel.

'Goppel, is it? I've never heard of any Goppel round here.'

'He lives with a chap called Lennon.'

'Ah! Toby Lennon, to be sure! You're looking for the pansy-boy. I can't say I've heard his name before. Their flat is the top of number fifteen.'

Number fifteen was a shop whose windows were entirely covered by posters advertising every kind of event from all-in wrestling to a meeting of the Parousia Society in preparation for the Second Coming. There was a passage at the side leading to a dark, uncarpeted staircase. Wycliffe climbed three flights to a landing with two doors on one of which the name 'Lennon' had been written with a felt pen. He knocked, and after an interval knocked again. There was a sound of movement and the door was opened by a slight, fair young man who stood looking at him in a vague uncomprehending way. Wycliffe introduced himself.

'Mr Goppel?'

'That's right.'

'May I come in?'

He followed the young man into a shabby, dusty living-room which smelled of mice and decaying food. Goppel was quickly recovering his self-possession and Wycliffe, who had suspected drugs, decided that he had merely been asleep.

'I've got some bad news for you, Mr Goppel.'

'Bad news? Not about Toby?' His voice was slightly higher pitched than is usual in a man and taken with his slim figure and almost feminine features it was inevitable that he should be labelled a queer whether he was one or not.

'Your father.'

'Is he dead?'

'Yes.'

'How did it happen?'

'He was found hanged in his house.'

'*Hanged*? You mean he committed suicide?'

'It looks like it. Have you any idea why he might have taken his own life?'

'Good God, no! He was all right when I saw him last.'

'When was that?'

'A week ago or a bit more, perhaps.'

'Did he mention that some papers and money had been stolen from his workshop?'

'No, he didn't say anything like that.'

'When did you leave home, Mr Goppel?'

'Just over two years ago.'

'And you came to live with Lennon then?'

'Yes, we've known each other since we were kids. He used to live in the Court, he was an orphan and he was brought up by his aunt, Mrs Hedley.'

'The Coles had come to live in the Court before you left?'

'Oh, yes.'

'So you remember Yvette?'

108

'Yes. That's the girl who's been murdered.' Two and two made four with an all but audible click. 'You can't think that's anything to do with the old man . . . ? Good God! Is that what you're saying?'

'No, I've no idea whether or not there is any connection between your father's death and the murder of Yvette.'

'But you think there might be?' His concern and distress struck Wycliffe as more or less normal but over and above these natural emotions he seemed inordinately scared so that he watched Wycliffe as a cat watches a strange dog.

'A small point, Mr Goppel, have you any idea where your father spent the occasional week-end away from home?'

'Fishing.'

'Fishing? I saw no tackle in the house.'

'He didn't bring it home; he was friendly with the landlord of the pub at Bickersleigh and he would go to stay there overnight sometimes.'

Wycliffe asked the inevitable questions and received stock answers. 'As far as you know, was anything worrying your father when you last saw him?'

'No, he seemed quite as usual to me.'

When Wycliffe had gone Freddie sat staring at the floor and listening for Pongo's step on the stair. He could not take in the magnitude of what had happened to him or foresee how his life would be affected. Without Pongo he was lost, not knowing what to think or do. But it was an hour before Lennon arrived and by that time Freddie was in a state of great excitement and had to be coaxed into intelligibility.

Joan Fiske was shelling peas for the evening meal. She was almost happy; first because she was relieved of a nagging fear; second, for a reason not so easily explained. It was not that she was vicious or that she

109

wished misfortune on others but when misfortune befell her acquaintances she could not help feeling that some vaguely conceived principle of justice had been vindicated. 'You see!' she told herself, 'you are not the only one who suffers. It happens to others.' And for once she looked forward to her husband coming home so that she could tell him the news and they could discuss it.

When he arrived he went upstairs without a word and by the time he came down she had the soup on the table.

'So they've found Yvette.'

He unfolded his napkin and tucked it in. 'They've found her body, if that's what you mean. Some yobbo she picked up with, I suppose. You could almost say she was asking for it.'

'No.'

'What do you mean – "No"?'

'It was Willy Goppel. He killed her then committed suicide. They found him this afternoon, hanging from his own staircase.'

Fiske paused with his soup spoon half-way to his lips. 'Ah!' He said no more for a moment or two, giving himself time to reflect. He was not a man to express an opinion lightly. 'Well, I can't say I'm altogether surprised. A man living alone, playing with kid's things.' After drinking a little of his soup he added, 'I've always felt that there was something not quite right about Goppel; in some ways he was too good to be true.'

'At any rate they can't come worrying Marty now, can they?'

'Marty? What's it got to do with him?'

Mrs Fiske realized that she had said more than she meant to. 'I don't know, I just thought that being like he is they might . . .'

'Don't be ridiculous!'

110

It was rare that they had a subject of mutual interest to talk about and Mrs Fiske was reluctant to let it go.

'What will they do now? Will there be a trial? They can't try a dead man, surely?'

'Of course not! The case will be allowed to drop. We shall hear no more about it.'

But for once Mr Fiske was wrong.

The Wards were having their evening meal, or to be more accurate they were sitting round the table though no one felt like eating. Alison had been crying, Henry was pale and silent.

Mrs Ward said, 'I just don't believe that Willy Goppel was capable of such a dreadful thing. I mean, you two children when you were younger spent half your time in there. You were in there with him more often than you were here with us, what with the shop and one thing and another . . .' She appealed to her husband, 'Do you think he could have done such a terrible thing, Edward?'

Mr Ward shook his head, 'It hardly seems possible.'

Franks sipped very dry sherry and put his glass down on the white, metal desk. 'Apart from the removal of her shirt there is no reason to see this as a sex crime. The girl was, in fact, a virgin. The scratches on her body were caused after death, presumably when she was pushed over the wall of the churchyard.'

Kersey was riding high in the company of a chief-super and a distinguished pathologist, full of bonhomie and chilled lager. 'If the murder and suicide are linked then Goppel must have killed the girl and if the motive was not sex it must have been something else. Perhaps it was Yvette who stole the cigar box from Goppel's desk. She seems to have had a free run of the place and it would account for the money I found in her room.'

'Do you think it was Yvette who sent you the papers?' Wycliffe looked at the sergeant with interest.

'It's possible. After all, she might have heard Geoff Bishop and her mother talking about me – they know me well enough.'

'But even if she stole the stuff and sent you the papers to pay off some grudge against Goppel, why did he kill her? The damage was already done.' Wycliffe turned to Franks. 'How exactly did she die? What sort of reconstruction can you make?'

Franks ran a pink hand over his thin hair. 'She died of manual strangulation, facing her attacker who, I feel sure, wore gloves. His thumbs met at some distance above her larynx and the hyoid bone was fractured. A good deal more force was used than was necessary.'

Wycliffe nodded. 'But that is common enough – you are not saying that her attacker was necessarily a strong man?'

'By no means.'

'You have seen Goppel's body, would you say that he was physically capable of having killed her?'

Franks looked puzzled. 'Of course.'

'But if she put up a fight? She was a healthy fifteen-year-old girl, small but wiry.'

'An oldish man of no great physique would have had difficulty.'

'Did you find any scratches or abrasions on Goppel's body?'

'None.'

Wycliffe sipped his beer. 'When her mother saw the body this morning one of her questions was, "Who cut her nails?" If they were cut by her killer it could only have been to make sure they held no tissue or fibres which might incriminate him.'

Franks laughed. 'In your usual roundabout fashion, Charles, you are saying that you don't think Goppel killed the girl.'

112

Wycliffe did not answer and Kersey said, 'In that case there is no connection between the murder and the suicide and I find that difficult to believe.'

Wycliffe sighed. 'So do I.' He glanced at the white digital clock on Frank's desk. 'It's gone ten, let's think about it again tomorrow.'

Outside it was raining and Kersey said, 'Change in the weather.'

'Where did you leave your car?'

'In Falcon Street, but don't bother, sir, I can catch a bus back.'

'Don't be daft, man.'

'A very decent bloke,' Kersey told his wife. 'The nearest thing I've found to a human being above the rank of inspector.'

'Perhaps this will help you with your promotion.'

'At my age? In any case, I don't know if I want it now.'

'Don't kid yourself, your eyes go green every time you mention it.'

When Wycliffe had dropped Kersey he went into the incident-van for a last look round before going home. Sergeant Bourne had taken over from Scales and a solitary D.C. was doing one-finger exercises on a typewriter.

Bourne was one of the new breed of policemen, weaned on computer print-outs; he was ambitious, a trifle arrogant, and Wycliffe did not like him though he conceded that he was a good officer. Bourne was working at Yvette's little diary.

'Found anything?'

'Nothing world-shaking, sir. The first thing that struck me was these asterisks which occur on consecutive days at intervals. They obviously refer to her periods. As to the initials, there are eight sets and five of these correspond to the names of the boys at her school with whom she was friendly. I got those names from reports of our people who made enquiries. Henry Ward seems to be referred to simply as "H".' Bourne turned the pages. 'The most interesting item is the figures which appear regularly each Sunday during the past twenty weeks – since April. Figures like 5.30, 5.50, 6.10 and so on. At first I thought they referred to times of appointments but some of them are much too precise – here, for example, 5.23. Nobody makes an appointment for 5.23. Not even me.' For once Bourne guyed himself.

'What are they then, money?'

'I think so. Money paid to her each Sunday. Perhaps she was doing a part-time job at week-ends.'

Wycliffe agreed. 'We'll put somebody on it in the morning.'

He got into his car with the intention of driving straight home but his way took him through the city centre, near La Cassandra in King Street. Almost before he realized what he was doing he had parked the car and was walking along the wet, deserted pavements in the direction of the club.

As always on Monday nights the city streets were dead and the flashing lights of La Cassandra were like an oasis in the desert, but inside business was slack. Although he had been in the place only once before, they knew him and he was not asked to show a membership card or to sign the book. The subtle communications system, rivalling ESP, which operates in such places brought Natalie through the curtained door from her office just as he entered the main room. Several customers were sitting at the tables, a few couples were slouching round the floor although the band was not playing. Instead, a slim, gamine-type girl, perched on a stool, was playing an accordion. She wore a sort of leotard which left one breast bare and she played moodily. The dancers seemed to ignore her.

Natalie came across the floor towards him. She was a beautiful woman; you couldn't blame any man for wanting to take her to bed and the wonder was that she had picked an oaf like Bishop for the privilege. The artful simplicity of her white gown and the candour of her dark eyes gave an impression of innocence which scarcely survived two minutes of conversation.

'Any news?'

Wycliffe said, 'I suppose you've heard about Goppel?'

'Yes, but you can't think he murdered Yvette? That funny little man? It's ridiculous!'

It was a novel experience, hearing a mother discussing the very recent murder of her daughter in this objective fashion. But Natalie had been raised in a realistic school.

'I want to talk to you.'

She led him to a table in a corner of the room which was even less well lit than the rest.

'Drink?'

'No, thanks.'

Natalie was keeping an eye on all that was happening, nothing escaped her.

'Where did Yvette get her money? Ninety pounds in the drawer in her bedroom and another ten in her handbag.'

'I've no idea unless she was going with men.'

'She was a virgin. Could she have got it from you without you knowing?'

'No way!'

'Bishop?'

A faint smile. 'Geoff would make Shylock look like a free spender.'

'Is it possible that she had a part-time job? Say on Friday and Saturday evenings?'

Natalie frowned. 'A job? I suppose it's possible. How can I know what she did with herself with me stuck here?'

Wycliffe had been watching the customers round the bar which was better lit than the rest of the room. 'Isn't that Freddie Goppel – third from the left at the bar?'

'Yes.'

'Is he a member?'

'No, but he comes in with the chap next to him who is.'

'The fellow with the black thatch?'

'That's right, Toby Lennon – known as Pongo. He and Goppel share a flat and they're more than a bit . . .' She twisted one finger over the other.

'And the third man, the one with the bandit moustache – is that Bishop?'

She looked at him oddly. 'Haven't you two met?'

'A pleasure in store. Does he spend much time here?'

'He comes in occasionally with Lennon but mostly he'd rather I didn't see what he's up to.'

'Anybody else I should know?'

She pointed to a table near the bar. 'That's Martin Fiske working late.'

A tall, well-made man in his early forties, beginning to go soft; over meticulously turned out; all deodorant and aftershave.

'Who's the girl?'

'You flatter her; she's thirty-four or five. She works in his office and he's set her up in a nice little flat in Parkeston.'

'Does his wife know?'

'If she doesn't she must be the only one.'

The accordionist had stopped playing and the dancers were drifting back to their tables. The girl in the half-leotard put her instrument in its case and tucked it away in a recess, then she crossed the floor to where Natalie was seated with Wycliffe.

'I was due off twenty minutes ago. Where's the group?'

Natalie glanced at her watch. 'They're not coming back – with this lot it's hardly worth it.'

The girl shrugged, totally unselfconscious of her skimpy costume. 'That's not my affair.'

'All right, you'd better go.'

The girl gave Wycliffe a backward glance as she made off to the dressing rooms.

Natalie sighed. 'I shall have to get rid of that little slut; she's too lazy to breathe and she solicits the customers.'

'How did Bishop get on with Yvette?'

'All right, why?'

'No problems?'

'None.' Natalie was fiddling with a glass ashtray, turning it this way and that. 'You don't think much of me as a mother and maybe you're right, but Yvette was difficult; she wouldn't be told. She had no room for me and despite what the books say it's not unusual for kids to take against their parents – especially girls against their mothers. I hated the sight of mine. But I tried to help Yvette, I really did.

'She lived in a fantasy world. You say she was a virgin and I'm not surprised. It fits. She wanted to play with fire and not get burnt. She wouldn't understand that you can't go round sticking out your chest and wiggling your backside and expect the men to say "pretty, pretty" and leave it at that. You have to live in the real world – deliver the goods or not advertise 'em. God knows I've warned her often enough and if she'd listened she wouldn't be where she is now.'

Oddly, in this strange outburst, Wycliffe detected the first sign of real emotion in Natalie. There was a catch in her voice and she had spoken with sincerity. This was her code – not the attitude of every fond mamma to her daughter but there was something to be said for it.

'It's unlikely that this was a sex crime.'

'Of course it was a sex crime, whether she was raped or not. Why else would a fifteen-year-old girl get herself murdered?'

Talking to Natalie was like talking to an experienced colleague in the force.

He sat with his elbows on the table, watching her, giving her time to recover her poise. In the end he said, 'Why don't you go over and have a word with Goppel and his friend?'

She looked at him, surprised and a little scared. 'Talk to them? Why should I?'

'Don't you sometimes have a word with your patrons?'

She stood up reluctantly, suspicious of a trap yet afraid to refuse. 'What do you want me to say?'

'Anything you like. What do you usually say?'

She crossed the room to the bar and joined the party. Lennon was effusive. Wycliffe could not hear what he said but he saw him put one arm round her waist and the other round Goppel, blandly possessive. Natalie glanced back uneasily; Goppel seemed sullen and unresponsive, Bishop looked worried. Wycliffe had seen what he had wanted to see and left.

That night Natalie was home early. By one o'clock business at the club had folded. Bishop was in bed but not asleep.

'What time is it?'

'Coming up for two.'

'What did the law have to say?'

'He wanted to know where Yvette got her money.'

'Well, where did she?'

'I can't think. She was a virgin, Geoff.'

'She must have had a job.'

Natalie had undressed and now she went into the bathroom.

'Did he ask about me?'

'What?'

Bishop repeated his question.

'When he saw you at the bar he wasn't sure who you were.'

118

'That sounds healthy.'

Natalie came back into the bedroom and sat at her dressing-table brushing her hair. 'Things seem to be running your way at the moment.'

'How do you make that out?'

'If Freddie Goppel comes into his father's property you should be all right. You seem to get on well enough with him.'

'He's a bloody poof.'

'What difference does that make? He's worth keeping in with.'

'Sure! I don't think we'll have any problem with him but I'm not so sure about his stable-mate.'

'Pongo? It's got nothing to do with him.'

Bishop turned over in bed. 'Don't kid yourself, little Freddie won't fart unless he asks Pongo first. That won't change.'

'Then you'll have to watch it with both of them.'

'I do, sweetheart, I do.'

Wycliffe drove home. Home was The Watch House, a former coastguard building of grey stone, solid and four-square. It stood on one of the two promontories which guarded the entrance to the narrows and funnelled all the maritime traffic of the port. The nearest house was a quarter-of-a-mile away and his wife, Helen, with his labouring assistance had turned half-an-acre of rough grass into a garden with rhododendrons, azaleas, camellias and magnolias, all shielded from the salt winds by a phalanx of tamarisk, olearia and senecio. From the road the house showed slightly paler than the darkness and beyond were the navigation lights of the channel and a gliding shape, pin-pointed with lights – a ship of some sort putting to sea.

Wycliffe's claims on life were tentative and his estimate of his entitlement was modest. He attributed what he had and what he was mostly to luck and he was often troubled by the thought that his slice was too large. Helen had no such qualms; she took hold of what was hers with both hands and fashioned it to her liking with infectious enthusiasm. But it was Helen who had grown to love music while Wycliffe found a bitter-sweet escape in the novels of Tolstoy and Balzac, Dickens and Trollope, Sartre and Simenon.

Helen was in the living-room surrounded by gardening books and catalogues, listening to the record player.

'What is it?'

He was being tested. She had taken his musical education in hand.

'Sounds like Mozart.'

'It's Haydn's London Symphony.'

'Oh, well, that's not so bad – if it isn't Mozart it's Haydn and if it isn't Haydn it's Mozart.'

'Nonsense!'

Was it all in the same world?

CHAPTER SIX

Henry Ward could not sleep and at first light he slipped out of bed and crossed the landing to his sister's room. He opened the door and the curtains billowed in the through draught from the window. He could hear the rain driving against the glass but Alison was asleep under the bedclothes, only her hair gleamed dimly in the pale light.

'Alison!'

She shifted her position but did not wake. He tried again and this time he touched her so that she was awake at once, startled. 'Oh, it's you. What's the matter, is something wrong?'

He perched on the edge of her bed. 'I've got to talk to you, Ali. I didn't tell the police the truth about Yvette – at least I didn't tell them everything I knew.'

She sat up in bed, pulling the bedclothes about her and yawning. 'Put on my dressing-gown, you'll freeze sitting there.'

He obeyed with unaccustomed meekness. 'I saw her on Saturday night.' His sister said nothing and he went on: 'When the policeman questioned me on Sunday I had no idea that anything really bad had happened, I thought she'd gone off somewhere to get away from her mother and I'd promised not to say anything.'

'Did she tell you she was going?'

'Well, she said she was going but I didn't think she meant right away.'

'You'd better start at the beginning, Harry, boy.'

'It's difficult. You know when her mother invited me

121

over for a drink – well, it was like . . . like we thought it might be.'

'You mean she wanted you to go to bed with her?'

'Yes.'

'And did you?'

'Yes.'

'Did Yvette find out?'

'She came in the front door as I was coming downstairs.'

Alison's warm hand searched for his and held it. 'Is that why you wouldn't come with us to London?'

'Yes. I wanted a chance to talk to her alone, to try to explain. I couldn't do it at school, you know what it's like there, and I couldn't risk going to her house. I tried to catch her in the evenings but it was obvious she was avoiding me. Then, on Saturday, when you'd gone to London, I spent most of the day looking for her. In the afternoon, about half-past three, I was in my room when I saw her going out of the Court through the archway. I dived downstairs and out into the street but I missed her –you know what it's like with the market people packing up.'

'So what did you do?'

'Well, I guessed she'd be making for the centre so I hared off up the street to the bus stop and I saw her getting on a bus but I was too far away to catch it. I walked in but of course I didn't know where she would go exactly. I stooged round the coffee bars then hung about waiting for the discos to open thinking she was bound to turn up somewhere like that. Around six I happened to be in Hilary Street – just killing time, walking – when I saw her ahead of me. She went down a flight of steps to a restaurant – a cellar place called The Catacombs. It was closed but there was a notice which said it opened at six-thirty so I hung about.

'It was an expensive place so I didn't like to go in but after it opened, each time somebody did go in, I tried to see through the open door and in the end I spotted her. She was dressed in a red dress with an apron and she was carrying a tray. She was working there as a waitress.'

'You didn't know she had a part-time job?'

'No, did you?'

'No.'

'Well, I thought I would meet her when she finished work and take her home but I couldn't stand there in the street for ever so I plucked up courage, put my head round the door and caught the eye of another waitress. She was a bit shirty but she told me that Yvette finished at ten. I spent the evening in the cinema watching some stupid film and got back to Hilary Street just before ten. She came out about ten minutes past and she was pretty mad to find me there but she calmed down and we walked through the quieter streets until we came to that bit of a garden in Lodge Road where we sat on a seat.

'She was miserable and very bitter about her mother and Bishop but she didn't seem to hold it against me – what had happened, I mean. She said that her mother hated her and wanted to take away everything she had. What had happened with me was the last straw. By this time she was crying and I felt very sorry for her. I tried to say the right things and cheer her up but I didn't manage it.'

'What happened?'

'Nothing, really. When she stopped crying she seemed to get more angry and she kept saying she was going to get even with her mother. I tried to get her to promise not to do anything silly. After all, I felt responsible for her, but all she would say was, "You wait! One of these days I shall just walk out!" '

It was getting lighter and Henry could see a shadowy outline of the dolls' house Willy Goppel had built for Alison. It seemed to belong on the other side of a great gulf and he shivered.

'You're cold!'

'No. Anyway, I told Yvette she must be sensible. With no money and nowhere to go she would just land herself in worse trouble. She said I'd be surprised how much money she had already and that she knew how to get more. She also made me promise that I wouldn't say anything *whatever* happened and she kept on so much that I had to promise.'

'What happened when you finished talking?'

'Well, I wanted to take her home but she wouldn't hear of it; she got almost hysterical when I insisted so I had to let her go.'

There was a break in his voice.

Alison said, 'But you weren't in love with her, were you?'

'No, I suppose not; but I liked her and now . . .'

For a time neither of them spoke and they sat listening to the rain on the window then Henry said, 'What am I going to do, Ali?'

In the strengthening light she could see his drawn, anxious features and the mild impatience she had felt seemed like disloyalty. She squeezed his hand. 'There's only one thing you can do; tell the police, and the sooner the better. Before school this morning.'

'You think so?'

'I'm sure so. I'll tell them at school that you'll be a bit late.'

'They might arrest me.'

'Don't be daft, Henry. Nobody will ever believe you could hurt anybody on purpose, not even a policeman.'

Henry got up, reluctant but resigned. 'I suppose that's the right thing to do.'

'Henry . . .'

He turned back. 'There's something I didn't tell the police about Yvette.'

'You?'

'Yes. Two or three times she talked to me about her sex life and she made out that she was going with men and getting money from them.'

'She was making it up.'

'That's what I thought, but you're quite sure?'

'Yes.' He hesitated for a moment before adding, 'She didn't really like anything like that.'

Kersey gave him a fairly rough passage. After Henry had told his story and been cross-questioned for upwards of half-an-hour, Kersey looked at him with great seriousness. 'So you were the last person to see Yvette alive – as far as we know.'

Henry was startled. 'No, of course not!'

'Then who was?'

'Whoever killed her.'

'And you did not?'

'Me? I've already told you she left me sitting on a seat in Lodge Road and said I wasn't to follow her.'

'We've only your word for that. For all I know you might have travelled back with her on the bus, taken her to the churchyard, tried to make love to her and when she resisted . . .'

Henry went pale. 'That's a terrible thing to say!'

'Why? Somebody killed her.'

'Yes, but I couldn't kill Yvette . . . I couldn't kill anybody. It's horrible! I've told you the truth—'

'But you didn't choose to tell it until you thought you were safe.'

'I don't know what you mean.'

'Until you thought her death was down to Willy Goppel.'

'That's not fair! I didn't tell you on Sunday because I'd promised Yvette and I thought she'd just cleared out. I had no idea that she was . . . that she was dead.'

'But you've known since yesterday.'

125

'Yes, but—'

Kersey cut him short. 'All I can say is it's lucky for you you weren't in love with Yvette. I hope you've learned something from mother and daughter.'

'I don't understand . . .'

The policeman laughed shortly. 'No, I don't think you do, but try working on it. Anyway, push off now, you can come back this evening and make a formal statement.'

'You mean I can go?'

'If you don't I shall probably kick you, but don't think you're off the hook.'

'At the door Kersey called him back. 'Do you think that Willy Goppel killed her?'

'No, I don't – I can't believe—'

'All right, get out.'

D.C. Dixon had been sitting-in on the interview. 'He could have done it, Sarge.'

'Him? He wouldn't stand on a snail. Anyway, this is no teen-age sex thing.' Kersey sighed, remembering something of what it was like to be seventeen, the poor goof in the middle, neither man nor boy, treading on eggs. 'Well, we know where she was until almost eleven o'clock on Saturday evening; that's something. You'd better check at The Catacombs and ask them if they never listen to the radio, watch TV or read a newspaper.'

'Sarge?'

'Why they haven't been in touch. Not that we can't make a good guess; they've been paying under the odds out of the till – no tax, no insurance, no come-backs.'

Despite the rain and the fact that Marty was miserable because he could not go beyond the verandah, Joan Fiske felt as though a great load had been lifted from her shoulders. Willy Goppel had murdered Yvette and hanged himself. It was incredible but she closed her mind to doubt. Now nobody would be likely to show any interest in the watch which she had hidden amongst her most private possessions in a locked drawer of the little bureau in her bedroom. Relief demanded action and she set about a thorough cleaning of the living-room, pushing the furniture about, dusting and hoovering.

Because of the noise made by the cleaner she did not hear anyone at the front door and she looked up to see Marty standing in the doorway of the living-room with the detective behind him. It was the man Kersey, the policeman who had called on Sunday, the day Yvette was missed.

'I'm in the middle of my work, Sergeant. I thought this whole dreadful business was over.'

The man looked surprised though whether his surprise was genuine or pretended she could not tell.

'What made you think that, Mrs Fiske?'

She felt a stab of renewed fear. 'What made me think it? Didn't Willy Goppel hang himself?'

'So?'

'Well, if he killed Yvette why do you still come pestering us? These people are nothing to do with us, they are just neighbours and we've told you all we know about them . . .' She broke off, conscious that the policeman was watching her with an odd expression. She had reacted too emotionally, she must calm down. 'I'm sorry there's nowhere to sit.' She gestured vaguely at the disordered room.

'It doesn't matter. I came to ask you about a watch, Mrs Fiske.'

'A watch?' It worried her that her question sounded flat and unnatural.

'Yvette was wearing a watch and it's missing.'

'What's that got to do with me?'

Kersey's manner was patient and unhurried. 'When I was here on Sunday, Marty came in asking something about a watch. It struck me at the time that you were

127

anxious to shut him up and get rid of me but I had no idea why until—'

'I don't know what you're talking about!'

He looked at her, not unkindly, 'It's no good, Mrs Fiske. As soon as I mentioned the watch you all but folded on me. I could question Marty, but I don't want to do that. He found it, didn't he?'

She was silent.

'Didn't he?'

'And what if he did? Marty wouldn't hurt a fly!'

Kersey was soothing. 'Nobody is suggesting that Marty hurt anybody, Mrs Fiske, but we've got to have that watch.'

Marty had lost interest and had gone back to the verandah. They could see him through the window, leaning on the rail, staring out at the rain. Joan Fiske left the room without a word to return a minute or two later with the watch, holding it by the bracelet.

'Here, take it! I wish to God I'd never seen the thing; I've hardly had any sleep since it's been in the house.'

'When did he find it?'

'On Sunday morning before you came, he showed it me while he was having his breakfast and I took it off him.'

'You knew who it belonged to?'

'I'd seen her wearing it. I thought she must have lost it in the Court and I was going to give it her back. It was only when you came . . . '

'You should have told me.'

She felt a sudden surge of anger against people who, like this policeman, had no conception what it was like to be watching, shielding, excusing and defending another human being throughout one's waking hours, each day and every day. 'How did I know you would believe that he'd found it? How do I know that you will believe it now? But he's a truthful boy, Mr Kersey; he never lies – *never*.'

128

Kersey nodded. 'I believe you, Mrs Fiske. So where did he find it?'

'I don't know; I didn't ask him, I wanted him to forget all about the damn thing.'

'Ask him now.'

She hesitated, but not for long. She called the boy in and he stood, looking from his mother to Kersey and back again, like an alert terrier anxious to do what was expected of him.

His mother pointed to the watch which Kersey was holding. 'I want you to tell me where you found it, Marty . . . No, you can't have it, it's not yours. I just want you to tell me exactly where you found it . . . Where did you find it?'

Her voice was quiet, soothing, almost hypnotic – quite different from the harsh tones and staccato sentences in which she carried on normal conversation.

Marty, having reached for the watch and been disappointed, allowed his arms to droop by his sides and stood listlessly.

'Where, Marty? Where?'

In the end, with a movement which signified resignation, he turned and led the way out of the room, down the verandah steps into the rain and across the Court until he reached a point near the steps which led up to Natalie's verandah. There he pointed at the ground and said, simply, 'Watch.'

His mother took him by the hand. 'You are sure, Marty?'

The boy had become indifferent and a trifle sullen but he nodded and repeated, 'Watch.'

Kersey was puzzled. Of course it was possible that the watch had slipped from Yvette's wrist at any time as she was coming out of or going into the house but it seemed unlikely that she would not have missed it at once.

129

With the watch in a polythene bag, Kersey returned to the incident-van.

'Is the chief in?'

The duty constable nodded. 'Number two, Sarge.'

Kersey found Wycliffe studying reports.

'Got something?'

Kersey slid the watch out of its polythene cover onto a sheet of white paper and explained how he had come by it.

Wycliffe produced a hand-lens and examined the bracelet. 'The catch looks sound enough but one of the little links between the charms has been pulled open leaving a sharp point almost like a hook.' He handed the lens to Kersey. 'There are a couple of fibres caught in the link – they could be wool.'

Kersey examined the bracelet with the lens. 'It might mean something but it's on the cards that Mrs Fiske has been keeping the thing with her winter woollies.'

'Anyway, get it off to forensic and see what they have to say.'

Kersey was leaving when Wycliffe called him back. 'About your interview with the Ward boy, I've seen the memo and I agree this is no teen-age crime but the boy's evidence is important and the sooner you get that statement the better.'

The implied rebuke was not lost on Kersey.

Wycliffe was left to his reports. Rain drummed on the roof of the van and streamed down the windows so that it was impossible to see outside. He skimmed through the forensic examination of Yvette's clothing – fifteen pages on six items – looking for a possible cherry in the cake.

'Dust extracted from the jeans and examined microscopically was found to contain sawdust, animal hairs, traces of bran, fragments of straw . . . '

In other words, at some time on Saturday, Yvette had

probably fed the animals and, perhaps, cleaned out their cages.

Another report, still more bulky, covered a detailed study of Willy's house and its contents, carried out by his own men. Only one point seemed worth making: the whisky glasses in the living-room both carried Willy's prints but one carried those of a stranger as well. The report included a blow-up photograph of the stranger's prints, marked, 'Not known', which meant that whoever he was he had no criminal record.

Wycliffe looked at the growing mass of paper and felt depressed.

Yvette was dead, Goppel was dead, and there seemed to be only two possibilities, one was that the two deaths were unconnected, the other, that Goppel had murdered Yvette then committed suicide. But Wycliffe was not satisfied with either. He could not believe that Paul's Court had been the scene of two unrelated violent deaths in a single week-end. On the other hand it seemed unlikely that a man of Willy's physique had murdered Yvette leaving no sign of a struggle. More than that, despite Kersey's speculation about a possible sinister side to Willy's character, Wycliffe could not see him as a child murderer.

A bizarre idea occurred to him. What if Goppel had been murdered? Murder by hanging, made to look like suicide ... The difficulties are so great that the mere possibility is usually disregarded. He glanced at his watch. Ten minutes past eleven. He could not expect a report from Franks until mid-afternoon but there was no reason why he should not look in to see how things were going.

Franks had his laboratory in the grounds of the City Hospital on the outskirts of the city and Wycliffe drove there through pouring rain. Car tyres raised plumes of muddy water from the streaming roads and windshield wipers worked overtime. He had difficulty in finding a parking space and when he did it was a couple of hundred yards away from the laboratory so that he arrived wet and feeling rather foolish at this exhibition of unprofessional impatience.

Franks was in his office working on the report with his secretary, surrounded by papers and photographs. Round and chubby, he sat at his desk, immaculate in a pearl-grey suit, striped shirt, mauve tie and with jewelled cuff-links just showing below the sleeves of his jacket.

'You've met Moira. Charles? . . . No? . . . Goodness! How time flies! Moira, this is Detective Chief Superintendent Wycliffe, my conscience. Without his silent disapproval I should be worse than I am. Charles is a rare bird these days, a dyed-in-the-wool puritan. I'm in the middle of dictating my report on your man, Goppel, Charles. Don't go away, Moira, unless you're going to make coffee.'

The girl picked up her notebook and went out smiling.

'I suppose there's no doubt he died from hanging?'

Franks spread his hands in a Gallic gesture. 'He was alive when his head went into the noose, dead when it came out, and he wasn't shot, stabbed, poisoned nor coshed.'

'No unusual features?'

'Unusual? What sort of thing?'

'I'm asking you.'

Franks picked up a coloured photographic enlargement and passed it over. The photograph showed the legs of the dead man from a little below the knees to the feet.

'Notice anything?'

'Nothing out of the ordinary. Post-mortem lividity and ecchymoses of the dependent limbs. Have I got it right?'

132

'You have, Charles, but look at the legs just above the ankles.'

Wycliffe held the photograph to the light and studied it more closely. 'The pattern seems to be very slightly different in a band round both legs.'

'Good! That's one of your unusual features though what it means I'm not sure.'

'A ligature?'

'It could be but it's too vague to build a lot on. Projecting the negative of that photograph I was just able to see a faint pattern of the man's socks imprinted on the skin in those areas but nowhere else.'

'What about the arms?'

Franks pursed his lips. 'There seems to be something just above the elbows but it's even more vague. However, look at this.' He passed over another photograph, this time in black and white. 'I suppose you could say that to some extent this has been faked. I printed it to emphasize contrast but it shows nothing that wasn't actually there.'

It was a photograph of Goppel's face in front view and it showed clearly the changes which death had brought about but there was something else, a pale area below the nostrils, extending down towards the chin and on both sides round the cheeks.

'A gag?'

The pathologist laughed. 'You said it. I wouldn't dare suggest such a thing in court without more to back it up.'

Wycliffe continued to study the picture. 'I see that, but taking it all together we have to face the possibility that Goppel was bound and gagged before his head was put in the noose.'

'Does that upset your calculations?'

'On the contrary.'

Moira came in with a tray. 'Black or white?'

Franks said, 'Old self-denial takes it black, he says he

133

prefers it that way.' He turned to Wycliffe. 'Murder by hanging, there can't have been many cases.'

Wycliffe sipped his coffee. 'Probably more than we think, we only know about the ones that were caught.' His mind was busy with the fresh evidence, trying to fit it into a pattern. 'One more point – was Goppel in good health before he died?'

Franks frowned. 'It depends what you mean, he was a good insurance risk, likely to live to a ripe old age, but I'd guess he didn't feel too good on the day he died.'

'Why not?'

'There was acute inflammation in the upper respiratory tract and a certain amount of congestion in the lungs. Almost certainly he was running a temperature. I'd say he had a dose of the 'flu which has been going the rounds recently. As you know, 'flu sometimes brings on fits of depression and if he did commit suicide that could have been a contributory factor.'

So Goppel had been bound and gagged before being hanged, which meant that he had been murdered. And at the time he had been suffering from a bout of influenza which would have made it easier for his attacker. Influenza . . . Yvette had been to the chemist with a prescription for an influenza mixture. If she had taken the medicine to Willy on her way home . . .

But how to prove murder? The evidence of the pathologist's photographs would not convince a judge and jury and the only chance of supplementing that evidence depended on the forensic examination of Goppel's clothing. If he had been tied up with some fibrous material – rope or cord, there was a chance that traces might remain, but the photograph suggested a strap and if this had been of leather or plastic there was little hope.

Back at the incident post Wycliffe telephoned the forensic laboratory and was put through to Clive

Horton, a scientific assistant with whom he had had dealings in another case. Horton was quiet, self-contained and competent, with the added merit that in court he could stand up to the roughest cross-examination without becoming in the least ruffled. He would repeat the same information over and over again in the most courteous manner possible until defending counsel or the judge tired of the exercise.

'Ah, Mr Wycliffe. I've been working on your man's clothing but I'm afraid I've nothing very helpful to report. Fine sawdust, traces of animal feed, animal hairs – predominantly cat, a few iron filings, wool and polyester fibres . . . '

Wycliffe said, 'I would like you to take another look with the idea in mind that he might have been tied up in some way. There is a suggestion that his legs might have been strapped together above the ankles and if so his arms were probably secured also.'

It was characteristic of Horton that he asked no questions not directly relevant to his work. 'You say that his legs might have been strapped together, presumably you mean strapped rather than tied?'

'Yes, a photograph of the legs shows a vague impression of a constriction about two inches wide just above the ankles.'

'I see. Of course much depends on the material such straps were made of. So far I have only examined samples of dust obtained by shaking out the garments separately in a polythene bag but I will certainly look at likely areas in more detail.'

'What about local creasing?'

'I don't hold out much hope there; the garments are made from materials containing a high proportion of man-made fibres and these are resistant to cold creasing.'

'Will you ring me when you have any further results?'

'I will ring you this afternoon.'

In the early afternoon Toby Lennon called on his aunt and uncle. Mr Hedley answered his ring; Mrs Hedley was in the kitchen washing up. For once, piano and radio were silent.

'Oh, it's you, Toby!' Mrs Hedley came out of the kitchen all smiles and kissed him on the forehead. 'What brings you here again so soon?' She reached for his coat. 'Let me take it. You're really *wet*! Why don't you get yourself a little car?'

'There's an obvious answer to that one, aunt.' He sat on the big Victorian sofa where, at this time of day, Mr Hedley should have been taking his nap. 'Freddie has gone to see Crowther at the Old Mansion House about his father's will.'

Mr Hedley hovered. 'How's he taking it?'

'Freddie? Well, he's upset, but he doesn't seem to realize what people are saying.'

'You mean that his father killed Yvette?'

'Yes. Is that what the police think?'

Mrs Hedley said, 'What else can they think? She was in and out of his house all the time, then she's found strangled and he commits suicide.'

Mr Hedley sighed. 'It's hard to credit all the same. I suppose this will make Freddie a rich man?'

'Perhaps; but there's no knowing how his old man left things. You know a bit about the law, uncle; if Freddie doesn't get anything can he contest the will?'

The old man laughed. 'Not a chance! Freddie isn't a dependent – or if he is he shouldn't be. If Goppel left the lot to a cats' home there's nothing Freddie could do about it.'

They were silent for a while; for some reason Mr Hedley's pronouncement seemed to have put a stopper on conversation, then Toby said, 'If the police think Willy killed her I suppose they will drop the case.'

'Bound to. A dead man can't be convicted of anything.'

Mrs Hedley was peering into a small gilt-framed mirror, trying to subdue her straggling hair by a redistribution of pins. 'Well, they hadn't dropped it this morning. That sergeant was with Joan Fiske for half-an hour and afterwards they came out with Marty in the rain and seemed to be searching for something on the ground outside the Coles'.'

'Searching for something, aunt?'

'That's what it looked like. I mentioned it when I was over there just before lunch but she was very tight lipped about it. There's something still going on.' She turned away from the mirror. 'I hope you don't mind, Toby, but I was going to listen to the Bartok string-quartet programme at three o'clock. Don't go away . . .'

Horton kept his promise and telephoned Wycliffe shortly after three. 'I've been over the trousers and jacket again using a vacuum extractor and taking separate samples from different levels on the legs and sleeves. The samples contained varying proportions of much the same materials as before but in three of them I found traces of something new. These were the samples taken from the trousers just above the ankles and immediately above the knees and from the jacket, above the elbows.'

Horton spoke in a dry monotone exactly as he would have given evidence in court. 'The new material is represented by very few fibres and I probably missed them in the earlier sample.'

Wycliffe was patient. 'Have you any idea what the fibres are or where they might have come from?'

'Yes, I have. Luckily I came across similar material in a case a couple of years back. They are cotton fibres, dyed with a greenish brown dye, and I am fairly confident that they came from cotton webbing of the kind once used by the Services for all kinds of slings, belts and straps. Government surplus stores used to be full of the stuff on haversacks, gas-mask carriers, water-bottle holders and goodness knows what.'

Wycliffe was pleased and said so. 'I suppose you've marked on the garments where the samples were taken?'

'Of course. The positions are consistent with the legs having been strapped together above the ankles and above the knees, while the arms appear to have been secured above the elbows. I will let you have my report tomorrow.'

Wycliffe thanked him and rang off.

There could only be one interpretation of the evidence now; Willy Goppel had been murdered by hanging. When and if the case came to court the defence would make a great deal of play with the difficulties of such a murder but Horton and Franks would prove unshakable witnesses, calm, never going beyond the facts, and never using two words where one was sufficient.

But it was premature to rejoice; he now had two murders on his hands instead of one and he was no nearer solving either. Still, truth is its own justification, or so they say.

On his way home that evening Wycliffe's mood was dismally philosophic. Somebody once said that right answers are easier to find than right questions. His questions had been, Who killed Yvette? Why? And why did Willy Goppel commit suicide? These questions had prompted some strange answers that were now irrelevant. The right questions seemed to be, Who killed Willy Goppel, and why?

Progress of a sort.

Yvette had walked off leaving Henry on the seat. She probably arrived back at Falcon Street shortly after eleven and Willy's back door was almost certainly unlocked. Knowing the place as she did, she would not bother to switch on the light in the workshop, enough light came from the stairs. It was easy to imagine her coming quietly through the workshop to the bottom of the stairs. Then, perhaps, she heard a sound. Did she call out? 'It's only me – Yvette!' Perhaps she looked up and saw the swinging body of the hanged man, but she must also have seen someone else – the murderer. Victim and murderer, both taken utterly by surprise, with no going back for either of them.

Did she scream? If she did there was no-one in the Wards' house to hear.

'In practice most murders fall into one of three main categories: domestic or family killings, killings incidental to robbery, and killings by homicidal lunatics.'

In his mind's eye Wycliffe could see the lecturer who had delivered himself of that pearl – on some course or other. And it was true, up to a point.

The man had gone on to say, 'Luckily for you chaps most murders are in the first category – arising out of the joys of family life and, after all, which of us would not cheerfully murder mother-in-law if we thought we could get away with it?' Pause for dutiful titter. Then, 'In such cases there is rarely any doubt about who did the job, it's just a case of finding sufficient evidence to convince a jury.'

Willy's death was certainly not the work of a homicidal lunatic; there was no question of it being a crime of violence committed in the act of robbery. That left domestic and family. Willy's only family seemed to be Freddie and Wycliffe had rarely seen a more improbable candidate for the dock on a double murder charge. Of course, there was Lennon, Freddie's simian friend.

Their relationship seemed to be as stable as many marriages so perhaps in these enlightened days Pongo could be looked upon as one of the family.

Motive? In domestic murders the motive is usually irrational – an explosion, a breaking point – but sometimes it is gain, and Willy was a wealthy man.

CHAPTER SEVEN

Wednesday. Yvette was to be buried in the afternoon and Wycliffe was going to the funeral. He had made an overnight statement to the press which, for once, appeared in the papers before it was mentioned on radio or television. *The News,* the city's own daily paper, came out with a headline on its front page:

HANGED MAN IN DOLLS' SHOP: MURDERED – OFFICIAL

Second Murder in Paul's Court

Last night Detective Chief Superintendent Wycliffe disclosed new evidence which makes it almost certain that Willy Goppel, the proprietor of the dolls' shop in Falcon Street, was murdered by hanging. Forensic scientists have been able to show that Mr Goppel was gagged and bound before his head was placed in the noose. It is believed that his bonds were removed after death to create the illusion of suicide.

Murder by hanging is rare in the annals of crime for there are obvious difficulties in persuading an able-bodied adult to place himself in a position to be hung. Cases are on record where the intended victim was either drugged or rendered insensible by a blow before hanging but such treatment would be unlikely to escape the notice of any pathologist.

In the present case the comparatively slight physique

of the victim and the fact that he was suffering from an attack of influenza certainly made the task of his murderer easier than it would otherwise have been.

In a telephone conversation with our reporter, Chief Superintendent Wycliffe mentioned another item of new evidence which may have great significance for both killings. In Yvette's handbag, found near her body, there was a bottle of influenza mixture which she had purchased from a chemist in the city centre on Saturday evening. It is known that Yvette was a frequent visitor to the Dolls' House shop where she helped to look after Goppel's collection of pet animals. The conclusion that she was taking the medicine to her friend is inescapable and it may be that this simple act of kindness cost Yvette her life. However, asked if he was satisfied that both murders had been committed by the same hand, Chief Superintendent Wycliffe said that he could not offer an opinion at this stage.

The report was accompanied by a photograph of a belt with a friction buckle and the caption read: 'A webbing belt as used by the armed services. The police believe that service webbing, easily obtained from government-surplus stores, was used to bind the murdered man.'

Wycliffe was at the incident post by eight-thirty, reading the newspaper report. Scales arrived shortly afterwards, followed a little later by Kersey.

'Sorry I'm late. I got stuck behind an RTA at Millbrook.'

The three men sat on bench seats round a small table to review progress and for the day's briefing. Outside the air was still moist from the night's rain but the sky was clearing, the sun had broken through and mists were rising from the sodden ground in the churchyard.

Wycliffe said, 'Now that we know Goppel was

murdered we must change our thinking. It seems that Yvette's murder was incidental to Goppel's and so we need to know a great deal more about him.'

It was agreed that Kersey should talk to the landlord of the pub at Bickersleigh where Willy had spent the occasional weekend. Scales would go through Willy's papers and see Crowther, his lawyer. Wycliffe said that he would call on Fiske who looked after his accounts. 'And I'll have a word with Natalie. She must have the low-down on a number of people who might interest us. Most of them seem to frequent that club of hers – Bishop, Lennon, young Goppel – and even Fiske. On the night I was there he was having an evening out with his secretary.'

Scales had left and Kersey was leaving when Fowler, the duty constable, came in grinning broadly. 'Visitor for you, Sarge, a Mr Alexander Chatham.'

Kersey looked puzzled then intelligence dawned. 'The Professor! What does he want?'

'He says he's got information concerning the death of his friend, Willy Goppel.'

'Does he now! In that case we'd better have him in.' Kersey looked doubtfully at Wycliffe.

Wycliffe got up. 'I can take a hint, he's all yours.'

The Professor came in wearing a black raincoat and carrying his Homburg, a furled umbrella crooked over his arm.

The Professor had an ambivalent relationship with the police and with Kersey in particular. Several times the sergeant had been on the point of nailing him for dishonest handling or 'fencing' but always the wily old boy managed to slip out from under. Far from bearing any malice, he had several times provided Kersey with useful information. Now he placed his hat and umbrella on a vacant seat and sat in the place Wycliffe had vacated. After fishing in the pocket of his raincoat he came out with a string of medals wrapped in tissue paper which he laid on the table for Kersey's inspection.

'German medals from the second world war, Mr Kersey. As you see, they include the Iron Cross and they belonged to my friend, Willy Goppel.'

'How did you get hold of them?'

'By the merest chance. I bought them in the ordinary way of business; Willy happened to see them on my stall in the Falcon Street market, recognized them, and told me that they had been stolen with other items from his workshop.'

'Go on.'

'I pressed him to take them back but he wouldn't hear of it. He said the medals were of no interest to him but he was concerned about certain papers which had been stolen with them. He enlisted my help to try to find out what had happened to them.'

'So you went to the chap for whom you had fenced the medals and asked him what he had done with the rest of the stuff.'

The old fellow was unperturbed. 'I bought the medals in good faith from a stranger who walked into my shop one afternoon. He said he had had them for a number of years and wondered if they were worth anything. I offered him twenty pounds, paid cash, and he left satisfied.'

'So you couldn't help Goppel?'

'Not so fast, Mr Kersey. I was anxious to do Willy a good turn and now that I knew that the medals had been stolen I simply put the word round. Few transactions are carried out in absolute secrecy as you well know.'

'What happened?'

'To cut a long story short, I found that the medals had already changed hands once before reaching me and that the transaction had taken place in a public house in Tolgate Street called The Fair Maid; you may know it.'

'I do, it's a regular thieves' kitchen.'

'Indeed? I do not frequent the place myself.'

'Is that all?'

'The man who sold them was not an habitué of the place but he had been seen there several times.'

'Does he have a name?'

The Professor hesitated only momentarily. 'Lennon – Pongo Lennon.'

'Lennon!'

'You know him?'

'I know of him.'

'Then you probably know that he shares rooms with Willy Goppel's son, Freddie, and you will understand why I dropped my enquiry at that point.'

Kersey was tapping the table with his ball-point pen. 'Well, I've got to admit, you've done us a good turn there. I shall want you to make a formal statement . . . '

'Don't you want to hear the rest?'

'There's more?'

'A little. On the following Saturday – last Saturday – I expected to see Willy in the market as usual but he did not come and it was evening before I was at liberty to visit him—'

Kersey leaned forward. 'You mean that you were with him on Saturday evening?'

'I was—'

'At what time?'

'I arrived around eight and left just after nine.'

'You realize that you could have been the last person to see him alive?'

'Apart from the killer, that is possible.'

'And you've only now got round to telling us about it?' Kersey's manner was menacing.

'If my friend had committed suicide nothing I had to say was of any importance.'

'But now?'

'If he was murdered, that is a different matter.'

'Tell me what happened on Saturday evening.'

'Not a great deal. Willy was not at all well, it was obvious that he was running a temperature – almost certainly it was influenza. We drank a glass of whisky together and I told him of my enquiries but I had the impression that he was not taking it in. I asked him if there was anything I could do – about the animals, about getting him food or medicine or some assistance.'

'What did he say?'

'He said that everything was taken care of, that the girl from next door had seen to the animals and that she was getting him some medicine from the chemist.'

'He was expecting her?'

'Yes. He told me that she would be looking in later in the evening. When I was leaving he said, "If you don't mind going out by the back door it will save me coming down. I left it unlocked for my little girl when she comes with the medicine."'

Kersey sat looking at the Professor for some time then he said, 'I'm going to put you in with D.C. Fowler and you're going to make that statement.'

Freddie Goppel, in slippers and dressing-gown, slouched across the living-room to the window, threw back the curtains and stared out over the grey roofs. 'Bloody hell!'

He ran his hand through his fair curls; he was pale and hollow-eyed. The room was damp and clammily cold. He crossed to the door, turned the key and went out to the landing where there was a pint-bottle of milk, a newspaper and an official looking letter addressed to him. He took it all inside and opened the letter which was from Crowther, his father's solicitor:

Dear Mr Goppel,

Thank you for calling on me, it is unfortunate that I was engaged at the time but I understand that my clerk was able to give you all the information you required. As your late father's executor I cannot proceed to obtain probate until I have either a death certificate or an equivalent document from the coroner's office. I understand from my clerk that you believe the police to be satisfied that your father took his own life; if this is so there should be little further delay.

May I say how deeply sorry I was to hear the sad news? Your father was a valued client and a near neighbour for many years and it was my pleasure to deal with his affairs personally.

Sincerely yours,

Arthur Crowther.

Freddie dropped the letter on the table and turned to the newspaper. The headline was ironic, a crushing retort to the presumption of the letter: 'Hanged man in Dolls' Shop: Murdered – Official'.

At first he did not take it in, the headline was cryptic; when he did he felt faint and had to hold on to the table for support. The sensation passed and he forced himself to read the whole report though he had to go over each paragraph more than once before he grasped its meaning. When he had finished he slumped into a chair and began to sob. Tears forced their way through his lids and he gave way to weeping.

There was a movement in the bedroom and Lennon came through wearing a brightly patterned dressing-gown. 'What's the matter, Freddie boy?' He went over and, gentle as a woman, ran his fingers through the curls. 'What's the matter, boy?'

Freddie made no response and Lennon continued to caress him until his eye caught the newspaper headline; his fingers remained in Freddie's hair but they were still.

After a little while he said, 'Well, it doesn't really change anything, Freddie; nothing could bring your old man back.'

Freddie shuddered. 'But it's horrible! To hang him like an executioner!' However, he dried his eyes and blew his nose in a grubby handkerchief then he sat back in his chair, looking up at his companion. 'Pongo . . . '

'Yes, Freddie?'

There was a long hesitation before he said, 'It wasn't you, was it?'

Lennon stiffened. 'What the hell do you mean? Of course it wasn't me! Why should I go for your old man, he never did me any harm.'

Freddie was all but inarticulate. 'Well, you might have thought . . . '

'What might I have thought?'

'Well, I shall probably get his money now and you . . . '

Lennon glowered. 'The young heir bit! Now I've heard every bloody thing! Christ, Freddie, if that's what you think you'd better piss off now!'

Freddie was contrite. He burst into tears again. 'Don't be mad at me, Pongo, I'm confused, I don't know what I'm saying. I'm sorry . . . Truly sorry . . . '

'So you bloody well should be.'

When Mr Hedley returned from the morning shopping he brought the newspaper as usual and after his wife had put away the purchases he spread it on the table and

148

pointed to the headline. 'It says here that Willy Goppel was murdered.'

'Murdered? What are you talking about? How could he be murdered? He hanged himself.'

Hedley merely pointed to the paper and his wife found her spectacles then read every line with close attention. When she had finished she looked up. 'Then somebody else must have killed the girl *and* Willy Goppel!' She returned to the paper and started to read the report again, hardly able to credit what she had read the first time.

Martin Fiske's offices in King Street were situated in a block belonging to one of the big insurance companies and he shared the third floor with a solicitor and an architect. The reception desk was in a room where three typists hammered away at their machines.

Over the telephone Fiske had said, 'I've got a hell of a morning but I could fit you in between eleven-forty-five and noon.'

Wycliffe arrived promptly at eleven-forty-five and was shown in at once. To reach Fiske's office he had to pass through another in which four of five oldish men and a middle-aged woman were at work, and he was shepherded by the young woman who had been Fiske's companion at La Cass.

Fiske sat back in his upholstered swivel chair, behind a clear desk, relaxed and prepared to approach business by way of tangential courtesies.

'I've heard a great deal about you, Superintendent.' He said this in the manner of royalty being gracious.

But Wycliffe got straight to the point. 'You know by now that Goppel was murdered. Obviously his business interests could be important to our investigation. I have come to you to get the broad lines of your relationship

149

with him, but if any detailed investigation of his affairs become necessary it will be in the hands of Inspector Scales.'

It was clear that Fiske was winded by this approach. He spread his white hands and his coat sleeves rode up sufficiently to show the gold links in his shirt cuffs. 'Well, Mr Wycliffe, what can I tell you? We cater for a number of Willy Goppel's in this city – that is to say for people who have business acumen and prosperous businesses but do not like ledgers and are frightened by forms which come in buff envelopes. We are more than accountants, we undertake the routine administration of any business which is not large enough to employ a competent and qualified staff. I don't mind telling you that Goppel's was my largest account.'

He paused and picked an invisible thread from the sleeve of his jacket. 'Willy was a remarkable man. I suppose you know that he married an English wife? . . . She died when his son, Freddie, was six and she left Willy a little property – a few houses scattered about the city and two or three shops in Alton Street – poor class property on the whole. But Willy, by judicious buying and selling, turned this into a little empire which at today's prices might be worth *half-a-million.*'

Fiske paused, as parsons do after mentioning the divinity. 'And all this without employing anybody directly. Crowther looks after the legal side, Cassells and White collect rents and arrange lettings, inventories etcetera, while we keep his accounts, see to his insurances, deal with the tax people and take care of investments. The surprising thing is that it works! Though whether it will continue to work with young Freddie is another matter. Willy had a fantastic grasp of detail, he wrote down very little but he forgot nothing. Fiona, my secretary, called him Mr Memory.'

The windows of Fiske's office reached almost to the

floor and though they were on the third floor, from where they were sitting Wycliffe could look down on passers-by on the opposite side of King Street.

'I suppose it was from here that you saw Yvette on Saturday afternoon?'

Fiske seemed surprised by the change of subject. 'Yes, as a matter of fact it was. Isn't it a dreadful business? To think that little Yvette . . .'

'Will you be going to the funeral this afternoon?'

'Oh, yes. One must. Although we are such an ill-assorted community there is a good deal of the old neighbourliness in Falcon Street. I am going home to lunch today then I shall pick up my wife and we shall go together. As a matter of fact that is why I am so pressed for time this morning.'

'I suppose you can make no suggestion as to who might have had a grudge against Goppel?'

Fiske frowned and studied his finger nails. 'I really can't help you there, Mr Wycliffe. To the best of my knowledge Willy was well liked and he was always scrupulous in his business dealings. I cannot imagine why anybody would want to murder him.'

'No, that seems to be the opinion of all the people who knew him. Incidentally, Mr Fiske, I don't know if Sergeant Kersey has asked you this already, but were you out late on Saturday night? If you were it's possible that you saw someone whose presence meant little to you at the time but might be important in the light of what has happened.'

Fiske shook his head. 'I do understand, Superintendent, but I was not out late on Saturday night.' He chuckled. 'And unlike our neighbour, I do not spend much time on my verandah.'

Wycliffe thanked him and left. Fiske saw him out and somehow managed to convey that the interview had been a waste of his time. One felt that he might enlarge

151

on the theme at the golf club or wherever he met with his peers. 'If that's how they set about a murder inquiry then . . .'

But Wycliffe was not entirely dissatisfied.

Wycliffe and Kersey had a snack lunch with a drink at The Sportsman's in Falcon Street, not far from the entrance to the Court. It was a good local, patronized at mid-day by many of the shopkeepers in the street. The landlord and his wife divided their time between the two bars and the atmosphere was intimate and friendly. The two men sat at one of the tile-topped tables and were able to converse in some privacy. Kersey recounted his interview with the Professor.

Wycliffe said, 'So, as far as we know, he was the last person to see Goppel alive.'

'Yes, but you couldn't take him seriously as a suspect. A spot of dishonest handling is the Professor's limit and he does that as much as anything for devilment.'

Kersey took a mouthful of veal-and-ham pie. 'As I see it, the most significant thing he told us was that Lennon had the medals. If he had the medals he must have had the papers; they were kept in the same old cigar box, and if he had the papers . . .'

But Wycliffe was not to be drawn. 'We'll see what Natalie has to say about the Lennon – Goppel set-up before we make any move.' He changed the subject. 'I suppose you haven't had a chance to get out to Bickersleigh?'

'Not yet, sir. I was going there this afternoon.'

'Good. I'm going to the funeral. We'll meet and see how it looks this evening.'

To Wycliffe's surprise, Yvette's funeral was no hole-in-a-corner affair but a real occasion. He approved, for he believed in ceremony and in the public celebration of private grief. One should be left in no doubt about who it is for whom the bell tolls and the dead should not be flushed away like sewage.

He joined the procession of cars as they formed in Falcon Street. It was an occasion which the whole neighbourhood had come to witness and it was none the worse for the presence of the press and even a television camera. The cemetery was on a slope above the west side of the city and from it one could look away across the docks to the open sea – on this day a silver plain in the sunlight.

They gathered round the grave and from a point a little higher up the slope Wycliffe looked them over. Natalie, discreet in a dark slim-fitting woollen dress; pale and fragile as a Meissen figure. Geoff Bishop by her side, like a bull in the show-ring, on his best behaviour yet wary; his suits were all loud and the best he could manage for the occasion was a black and white check from which he bulged so that it would have been no surprise if the buttons had scattered from his jacket at any moment. Beads of sweat formed on his forehead to trickle down his cheeks and from time to time he wiped them away with a grubby handkerchief. The Wards: Henry with his sister, looking after her with the earnest devotion of a lover. Some girls have to live up to their mothers-in-law; Henry's wife, when he found one, would always suffer in comparison with his sister. Alison seemed unable to take her eyes off the coffin. Perhaps it was her first funeral, perhaps when it came to the point she could not quite believe in mortality – not for the young anyway.

In the second rank Mr and Mrs Hedley, looking as though they were being exposed to the air after a long period of incarceration, grey wraiths who must be thinking of their own final tryst. Then there was Martin Fiske with an expression on his heavy features which suggested that he would have organized the whole thing

153

differently, and his wife Joan – who darted quick, nervous glances about her almost as though she feared being attacked at any moment. Wycliffe wondered who was looking after Marty.

Pongo and Freddie offered their own particular version of the Yin and the Yang . . . Even the Professor was there, the only mourner distinguished by being dressed wholly in black. And there were others, strangers to Wycliffe, one or two of them with a foreign look, probably people from La Cass.

When it was over and the vicar was condoling with the principal mourners, Martin Fiske came over to Wycliffe, blandly importunate, 'Ah, Superintendent! If you are returning to your base in the churchyard, I wonder if you would be good enough to drop my wife off? It would save me having to drive her home and then return to the office. I've lost so much time today already . . . '

'I shall be glad to take Mrs Fiske home.'

'Ah! I knew you would oblige – most kind.'

Joan Fiske stood a yard or two away, passive and resigned, like a parcel awaiting collection.

'Here you are, my dear, the superintendent will take you home.'

She walked with Wycliffe to where his car was parked. He tried to make conversation but at first it was heavy going – until, apparently, the inhibiting effect of her husband's presence had had time to wear off. Then she gossiped freely enough about the Court, about Falcon Street and about her neighbours.

'You must have lived in the Court before young Goppel and the Hedleys' nephew left home . . . '

'Yes, long before. We moved in when the houses were new – at the same time as the Hedleys. That's ten years ago. The place suits us, you see. With Marty as he is

154

it's such a blessing to have the Court, it's secluded and it's *safe* and it's not too far from the city centre.'

'I can see that . . . I gather Lennon was an orphan?'

'His parents were killed in an air crash when he was ten and his aunt brought him up. His father must have been fairly well off for it seems he left money enough to keep Toby and send him to a public school, and when he came of age he had a little nest egg of several thousand pounds. Of course he spent most of it in the first year . . . '

It was obvious that Mrs Fiske rarely had an opportunity for gossip and she revelled in talking to this grave, courteous policeman who listened and nodded and asked questions as though he had a real interest.

'I gather that he doesn't have a regular job?'

'Indeed he doesn't! Work and Toby have never agreed; the nearest he ever came to it was a few years as an all-in wrestler.'

'A *wrestler*?'

She laughed – a rare phenomenon. 'Yes, a wrestler. He was mad on it. During his school holidays he used to spend most of his time at the gym in Wesley Street and when he left school he took it up. Of course, that upset his aunt. I suppose he must have become a professional for he used to appear on the television now and then. That was when he started calling himself Pongo – Pongo the Apeman and he used to come into the ring dressed like Tarzan and letting out blood-curdling yells.'

'What happened? Did he get tired of it.'

'No, I don't think so. I think he hurt somebody badly and he wasn't allowed to wrestle any more. Anyway, he hasn't done a stroke of work since of any sort.'

'And I suppose the Hedleys got fed up with keeping him?'

She denied this with some vigour. 'Oh, no! At least she

155

didn't. I don't think anybody ever asks Mr Hedley's opinion about anything. Mrs Hedley doted on the boy – and still does. If you ask me she still helps to keep him in idleness which is a shame because they can't have a lot.'

She lowered her voice. 'Toby left home because he's *peculiar*.' She would not use the word 'queer'. 'Of course, he couldn't carry on like that at home so he had to find a place of his own. Then it wasn't a great while before Freddie Goppel joined him.'

She broke off as the car turned under the archway into the Court. 'It's very good of you to bring me home like this. What was I saying? Oh, yes, about Freddie – I've never had much of an opinion of Freddie, he's a weak creature at best, but there's no doubt Toby corrupted him and I know his father felt very bitterly about it.'

Wycliffe felt deeply sorry for this neurotic woman, burdened with a retarded son and starved of companionship. When he got out of the car and opened the door for her he tried to say something vaguely consoling. She stood beside him for a moment as though reluctant to break the contact then, as she was turning away, she said abruptly. 'There's a murderer in this Court, Mr Wycliffe; you know that, don't you?'

Wycliffe shook his head, 'No, Mrs Fiske, I don't know.'

She was about to say something further when another car came through the archway. It was Bishop in his Cortina, with Natalie beside him, returning from the funeral. Mrs Fiske watched them while Natalie got out of the car and said a word to Bishop who then drove off again. Natalie went up the steps to her front door and let herself in with a key.

'I expect Mr Kersey told you that Marty found Yvette's watch right by those steps. Don't you think that's odd?'

Before Wycliffe could reply she was moving away

again. 'I must get indoors, I've got a friend keeping an eye on Marty.'

Wycliffe let her go.

After a moment or two he walked across to Natalie's house and rang the bell. He had to wait a little while and when Natalie came to the door she had changed from her mourning dress into a housecoat.

'Oh, I wondered if I was to have a visit.'

'I'm sorry to intrude, I realize it's not the best time . . . '

'No, but I'm not like a normal mother, am I? You'd better come in.'

As he passed her it was obvious that she had already been at the whisky. In the living-room there was a used glass on the drinks table.

'Will you have one?'

'Not now, thanks.'

'Well, what do you want?'

'I want you to tell me about some of the people who use your club. My only excuse for coming to you now is that you probably know them better than most.'

She perched herself on the arm of one of the big chairs. 'I wouldn't quarrel with that. You'd better sit down.' She pulled the skirts of her housecoat round her knees. 'Which ones do you want to know about? Some of them are not so bad, for others I can only think of four-letter words.'

'Freddie Goppel?'

'Freddie? He's a non-starter; he doesn't exist until bat-man pulls the strings.'

'I suppose you mean Lennon?'

She nodded. 'His big, bad friend.'

'Is he bad?'

'I don't know. I think he could be vicious in a tight corner. He's got a big mouth when he's had a few.'

'What about Fiske?'

She looked at him with fresh interest. 'Fiske? You're bringing it a bit near home, aren't you?'

'Do you mind?'

She took a cigarette from a box on the table and lit it. 'No, I don't mind. As a matter of fact Fiske is a client I'd just as soon be without. He's like a dirty minded kid.' She blew a perfect smoke-ring and watched it broaden and rise. 'Let's say I reckon his secretary earns her flat and whatever else she manages to get out of him.'

Wycliffe said, 'You understand I've only one interest in this, to find a killer.'

'So?'

'Coming nearer home still; what about Bishop?'

She did not answer at once and Wycliffe thought that she might take refuge in indignation but she remained calm and matter-of-fact. 'If I thought Geoff had killed Yvette I wouldn't hesitate to say so. He's got a temper and he might do anything when he's really roused but he'd be incapable of planning to kill anybody. Does that tell you what you want to know?'

'Yes, I think it does.' Wycliffe took out his pipe. 'Do you mind?'

'Feel free.'

'One or two more questions. Did Willy Goppel's name ever crop up in conversation at the club – I mean before he died.'

She nodded. 'Sometimes. You see Freddie spends quite a bit of time there and everybody knew his old man had money so there was a bit of leg-pulling.'

'Is that all?'

'No. There was something a week or two back. It was one evening, early, before the customers started to arrive. Toby Lennon was there, without Freddie for once, and he was drinking doubles with Geoff. He'd had several and, as usual, he was convinced he was the life and soul of the party. I think it was Stefan, the barman, who asked Toby where his friend was. I forget what Toby said but the conversation got round to Freddie's father being a German Jew and then there was talk about the Nazis and concentration camps. Toby was well away and he told some ghastly yarn about what they did to Jewish girls in the camps. It made you want to throw up but Toby doesn't like women and he goes for that sort of thing. To change the subject I asked if Freddie's father had been in a camp and somebody said he had.'

'Was that all?'

'No. Toby, without saying a word, took a wad of old papers from his wallet and spread them out on the bar. They were all yellow and practically falling apart and they were printed in German with some ordinary writing and two or three official stamps. When he had everybody watching, Toby said, "Willy Goppel, my children, is an old fraud; he's no more Jew than I am and he's certainly never been in a concentration camp. He was a captain in the German army with a string of medals to prove how good he was." Then he read out a lot of stuff in German which nobody understood.

'Somebody asked him where he got the papers and he made a mystery out of it though it was obvious he must have got them from Freddie. I don't think anybody was all that interested and it fell rather flat. Customers were beginning to arrive so he put the papers away, but just at the end he said to me – you know what his sort are like when they're drunk – "The next time you see Willy Goppel, you say to him 'Guten Morgen Herr Hauptmann' and see how he takes it.'

'He made me repeat it after him once or twice until I had it right. I did it to humour him because I didn't want a scene.'

'Did you try it on Goppel?'

She smiled. 'I did, as a matter of fact. I didn't mean to

but he happened to be standing under the archway one morning while I was in the car, trying to filter the traffic and it just occurred to me.'

'What effect did it have?'

'I don't know; it happened that at that moment I had my chance to move out.'

'You heard no more about these papers of Goppel's?'

She crushed out her cigarette in an ashtray. 'Yes, I did. Pongo – Lennon, that is, came to me next evening and said he'd had his wallet nicked with the papers in it. The fool had taken off his coat and slung it over a chair. I told him that if he'd lost them it was his own fault.'

CHAPTER EIGHT

'Well? How did you get on at Bickersleigh?'

Kersey grimaced. 'Nothing startling but it wasn't altogether a wasted trip and the beer was good. Apparently Willy and the landlord had been friendly since before Willy's wife died and I gather he went there more for companionship than for the fishing.'

It was early on the evening of the funeral and Wycliffe and Kersey were comparing notes in one of the cubicles of the incident-van.

'I got one or two tit-bits. Bishop's property at Fenton Street was leased from Willy and Willy had given him a year's notice of termination.'

'Did you find out why?'

Kersey grinned. 'I did. Willy was going to turn the place into a Disneyland for kids.'

'A *Disneyland*?'

'Well, not on that scale, but a place where the kids could meet the characters from their story books and from TV, in the flesh, so to speak. He had great ideas – all sorts of mechanical models, visits from prominent entertainers and goodness knows what.'

'It would have cost a bit.'

'Apparently that didn't bother him. He was prepared to realize some of his capital to pay for it and in any case he saw it partly as a business proposition. He was going to sell children's books, records and toys and there was to be a small charge for admission to the exhibition area. He realized that he would have to subsidize it but he told Victor – that's the landlord, that he might as well spend his money that way as leave it for Freddie to squander.'

'Interesting. Anything else?'

'Only that he hated Lennon's guts and blamed him for turning Freddie into a queer.'

When Kersey heard from Wycliffe that Lennon had been showing off Willy's papers at La Cass, he was predictably impressed.

'So now we have proof that Lennon had both medals and papers. It seems to me that whoever had possession of those papers and sent them to me, arranged Goppel's faked suicide and murdered Yvette when she caught him at it.'

Wycliffe said nothing and Kersey persisted, 'Don't you agree, sir?'

Wycliffe's answer was indirect. 'Whoever killed Goppel planned the crime very cleverly to look like suicide. The papers were sent to you; naturally you had to confront Goppel with them and take some action, but as soon as you did so you were providing a reason why Willy might become depressed and take his own life. We have already agreed that if it hadn't been for Yvette's murder it's very doubtful whether Goppel's death would have aroused any suspicion of foul play.'

Kersey allowed himself a show of impatience. 'What you are saying, sir, is that Lennon is a clever bloke. He probably is, he had a good education and I've no doubt he's intelligent.'

'But fool enough, apparently, to draw attention in advance to papers he proposed to use in an ingenious murder scheme. Fool enough too, to cash in on those medals and so risk everything for the sake of a few pounds.'

Kersey rubbed his bristly chin. 'As far as showing off the papers is concerned, Lennon was drunk and he made a fool of himself. He must have realized it for you say he was back the next night complaining to Natalie that he'd had his wallet nicked.'

'Perhaps he was telling the truth.'

Kersey's expression made it clear that he was having thoughts which cannot be expressed to a chief superintendent. 'Surely, sir, it's obvious he was trying to cover himself.'

Wycliffe smiled. 'At any rate, I agree that we should talk to him.'

'Shall I have him brought in?'

'No, we'll go and see him, we might get more out of an interview with his friend Goppel looking on.'

Telfer Street was utterly deserted, stoically awaiting the arrival of the demolition men. It was dusk and there was a light in the Irishman's shop. He came to the door as they passed.

'Nice evening, Superintendent. I think your friends are at home, they don't go out until a bit later as a rule.'

They climbed the three flights of stairs in almost total darkness. Kersey knocked on Lennon's door which was opened by the man himself.

'Freddie! You've got visitors.'

'It's you we've come to see, Mr Lennon, but Mr Goppel can stay if you have no objection.'

'Me?' Lennon's surprise was exaggerated. 'What can you possibly want with me?'

They followed him into the living-room where Freddie was in the act of turning off the television. He looked at the two policemen as though they had come to carry him off to execution.

'May we sit down?'

'By all means, gentlemen! This is Liberty Hall. You have a choice of a chesterfield with loose stuffing or an armchair sprung by a sadist.'

163

'I understand that you read and speak German, Mr Lennon?'

'I do, Superintendent. You see before you the product of an expensive public school education.'

Seen at close quarters Lennon was even more hairy and shaggy than Wycliffe remembered. His features, surprisingly pink and youthful, emerged from the undergrowth like geological outcrops in a forest.

'So you were able to read Willy Goppel's papers, and it seems that you did just that to several people at La Cass. On that same evening you coached Natalie to address Goppel as "*Herr Hauptmann*".'

Lennon laughed without much conviction. '*Guten Morgen Herr Hauptmann* – I was pissed, my dear Superintendent. It was a lark.'

'But you had discovered that Goppel was not the person he pretended to be for more than thirty years.'

'So what?' He looked sideways at Freddie who had been following the exchanges with nervous intensity. 'As I said, I was drunk and I did it for a giggle. Who cared after thirty years?'

Freddie seemed on the point of saying something but changed his mind. Kersey took over.

'Why did you send those papers to me if you thought they were of no importance?'

Either Lennon was startled by the question or he put on a good act. 'Send them to you? Why should I do that? To be honest, I'd never even heard of you until a day or two ago. And, in any case, I've no great liking for the genus copper.'

'They were handed in at the Mallet Street nick by somebody last Thursday, addressed to me. We know that you had them so if it wasn't you who handed them in, who was it?'

'A good question, with no answer as far as I'm

concerned. I lost the damn things; more accurately they were nicked along with my wallet.'

'What about the medals?'

'What about what medals? Or, perhaps I should say, What about which medals?'

Wycliffe said, 'We don't want to lay traps for you, Mr Lennon, so I will tell you that last Thursday Mr Goppel told Sergeant Kersey of the theft from his workshop of a cigar-box containing the papers, some war medals and a sum of money. Mr Goppel refused to make a formal complaint so the theft cannot be the subject of a charge. However, you should know that we have evidence that you sold the medals in the bar of The Fair Maid in Tolgate Street and they have since been recovered.' Wycliffe paused and turned to look at Freddie who shrank in his chair. 'Almost certainly Mr Goppel refused to make a complaint because he thought that the box had been taken by his son.'

'I—' Freddie began to speak but choked on his words.

Lennon was sitting on a cane chair which protested at every movement of his massive body. 'I don't get all this. You say that there is no question of a charge, so why all the fuss? A chief super and a detective sergeant chasing a few medals . . . '

Wycliffe's expression did not change. 'We are not interested in the medals or in the papers except in so far as they are linked with the murders.'

Lennon glanced quickly at Freddie and back again to Wycliffe. 'I don't see the connection. What have the papers got to do with the killings?'

'A good deal. Goppel's death was made to look like suicide and the suicide was made credible in advance. The papers were sent to Mr Kersey with a note saying they belonged to Goppel. Naturally he went to see Goppel and as a result the papers were forwarded to the

Home Office. Shortly afterwards Goppel was found hanged. On the face of it the business had preyed on his mind and he had committed suicide.'

For the first time Lennon showed real concern. 'There's been nothing about this in the paper . . .'

'No, but those are the facts. Had it not been for Yvette Cole becoming involved and losing her life in consequence, the verdict on Goppel would almost certainly have been suicide.'

There was a long pause during which Freddie startled everybody by a sudden, almost convulsive movement in which he tucked his legs under his bottom so that he was sitting in his chair Buddha-like.

Wycliffe gave Lennon time to think. Although he behaved like a clown it was clear that he had more than enough intelligence to calculate the score. It did not take him long.

'In the first place I wouldn't have been such a fool as to flash those papers round at La Cass if I intended to use them in some cunning plot – would I?'

'I've no idea. You say yourself that you were drunk.'

Kersey interrupted. 'You say those papers were nicked with your wallet. All right! Where? When? How?'

Lennon took a deep breath. 'As to where and when, it must have been at La Cass on that same evening. All I know is that I had them when I was playing the fool at the bar and I didn't have them when I got back here. My wallet was gone, papers and all.'

'You mean that you were dipped by somebody at the club?'

'I must have been. As I told you, I was a bit far gone and when customers started to arrive Natalie put me at a table near the back. I remember I thought it was bloody hot and I took my jacket off and hung it on the back of my chair.'

'Was anybody with you?'

'Geoff Bishop was told to keep an eye on me, to make sure I didn't disturb the customers or puke on the carpet. Then, Lisa, one of the girls, brought me a cup of black coffee and after that I felt better.'

'Did you tell Natalie about your wallet?'

'I did the next day but she said it was my own fault and there was nothing she could do about it.'

'Are you prepared to put all this in a statement and sign it?'

Lennon ran a hand through his mass of black hair. 'Why not?' He looked from Kersey to Wycliffe, 'Is that all?'

'Not quite. Where were you, say, between Saturday afternoon and the early hours of Sunday morning?'

He took time to consider. 'Well, I was in all Saturday afternoon watching sport on TV. In the evening Freddie and I went to a boozer—'

'Which?'

Lennon grinned. 'The Fair Maid.' He was recovering his nerve. 'We stayed there until round nine then Freddie went home and I toddled along to a party which wasn't Freddie's scene.'

'Where was this party?'

'A place belonging to an old mate of mine in Grenville Road. Chap called Hobson – Jeremy Hobson, number twenty-six.'

'What time did you get there?'

'Half-nine? Thereabouts anyway.'

'And when did you leave?'

He chuckled. 'Good question! It must have been in the early hours of the Sabbath. All I know is I had a thick head next morning.'

'Have you got a car?'

'Where would I get a car? I've got a push-bike and, believe it or not, I rode it back here.'

'One or two more points, Mr Lennon. I would like you to agree to a simple medical inspection.'

167

'What the hell for?'

'I assure you that it's necessary.'

'All right, as long as it's on the National Health.'

'And I want you to allow Mr Kersey to search this flat.'

'Will all this let me off the hook?'

'It will help.'

'Okay, if it amuses you. Anything else?'

'What clothes were you wearing on Saturday night?'

Lennon grinned. 'Well, it wasn't white tie and tails. A pair of M & S slacks and a blazer.'

'We should like to borrow those clothes and the shirt you wore.'

When Wycliffe was leaving Kersey followed him out on to the landing. 'Bloody clown! Do you think he's stringing us along?'

'I've no idea. You know what to do?'

'I think so, sir. Anything special in the flat?'

'Webbing, nylon cord, buckles, fastenings which might have come from Service webbing . . . Your guess is as good as mine.'

'He seems altogether too pleased with himself for my liking.'

Wycliffe said, 'I'll send a car to pick you up here and I'll make an appointment with the police surgeon for say, seven o'clock. If that's not possible I'll get a message to you.'

Back in his car Wycliffe contacted headquarters on the radio and gave the necessary instructions.

He drove back to Falcon Street well aware that he had made little real progress; it seemed unlikely that a case could be made out against Lennon on present evidence. So where did that leave them? Was there a credible alternative? Who wanted Goppel out of the way sufficiently to plan and execute such a hazardous crime? The stack of paper which the enquiry had accumulated carried one clear message: people liked Goppel, at worst they regarded him as eccentric, perhaps a little cracked. There seemed to be only one man with a real grievance – Bishop, but would Bishop murder a man over the renewal of a lease?

However, somebody must have wanted Goppel dead. Wycliffe remembered a Simenon in which Maigret had to keep reminding himself, 'Harry Brown is dead!' Well, Willy Goppel was dead too, and in very odd circumstances.

Kersey was hoping to find answers to three questions: was there anything incriminating in Lennon's squalid little flat? Did he have suggestive scratches on his body? Could his account of how he had spent Saturday night be regarded as an alibi?

Lennon appeared to be completely indifferent to the search of his flat. He sat on the ancient chesterfield reading a magazine while Kersey poked into every murky corner. By contrast, Freddie never let Kersey out of his sight, watching him as though in dread of some imminent catastrophe.

'What are you looking for?'

Kersey said, 'I don't know. Do you?'

'*Me?*'

Lennon was playful. 'Finished already?'

'For the time being.'

'Well, feel free, any time.'

And the medical got them nowhere. When Lennon left the police surgeon he was as jaunty as ever. 'What was the old leech looking for? Did you think I doped? Or spent my nights with poxy women?'

Kersey was not amused. 'Don't pretend to be more stupid than you are.'

Wycliffe had sent young D.C. Dixon with a patrol car to pick him up.

'Are you through, Sarge?'

'Through is the word. But we'll take a look at his alibi which will have more holes in it than a bloody colander.'

Grenville Road was tree-lined with the odd Mercedes, Jaguar or Rover 3.5 left nonchalantly in driveways. Number twenty-six was detached with enough garden to be self-supporting if ever the stock market really dived. It was growing dark, lights were on in many of the houses and there was that late evening stillness when people speak in low voices yet are heard at a distance. Kersey rattled the clapper of a bell on a wrought iron bracket, and the varnished door, studded with iron nails, was opened on a chain; the chain was unhooked when he poked his warrant card through the gap.

'What do you want?' Young and blonde with nothing visible on but a red velvet pinafore dress and a pair of peep-toe sandals.

'Mrs Hobson?'

'Yes.'

'You had a party here on Saturday night?'

'We did. Does that concern the police?'

'Only indirectly. As a matter of routine we have to check a statement made by a witness that he spent a good deal of Saturday evening and night here.'

'Does this person have a name?'

'Toby Lennon.'

'Oh, God! I might have known.' She sighed histrionically. 'What has he done?'

Kersey had the impression that Pongo was not among her top ten party guests. 'Nothing as far as we know.'

'Well, he was here.' She seemed to think that was all that was needed and was about to shut the door again.

'We would like as many details as you can give us and also your husband's recollection.'

Resignation. 'You'd better come in then. Does it take

two of you to do this sort of thing? I thought there was supposed to be a shortage of policemen.'

She showed them into a very large lounge where there were zebra-striped settees and armchairs on a pure-white carpet. The walls were creamy white and spotted with Bridget Riley abstracts which made the eyes go funny. 'White,' thought Kersey, 'is in. I must tell Esther.'

'I'll fetch my husband.'

When she had gone, Dixon muttered, 'A bit different from Telfer Street.'

'At home anywhere, our Pongo,' Kersey said.

The blonde returned with husband; perhaps a little older than Lennon, fair and slight, of aristocratic mould and manner. Out of Debrett by the skin of his teeth.

'Molly tells me that you are asking questions about Pongo Lennon. We were at school together.' He seemed to think some explanation of their association was needed. 'Saturday night was a bit of a riot, one of those parties where one evens up the score with a lot of people – pays off one's social debts in one fell swoop, as it were. We must have had upwards of fifty people here at one stage. Pongo arrived between nine and ten – before ten anyway – wouldn't you say, Molly?'

'If you say so.' Molly wasn't interested; seated on the white carpet, showing a great deal of thigh, she played with a cat who matched the carpet so well as to be almost invisible except when one glimpsed the dark nostrils and green eyes.

'Have you any idea how long he stayed?'

'Right through. Pongo never misses free booze if he can help it.'

'But you didn't see him all the time?'

'Not every minute, naturally; but I saw him pretty often and he was certainly among the last to go at about

171

three in the morning. I had to lever him out. Actually I had a pang of conscience. I said to him, "Have you got a car outside?" and he said, "No, old boy, but I've got my bike." Of course he was stoned.'

'Does that square with your recollection, Mrs Hobson?'

'Near enough; he seemed to be about, rather too obtrusively for comfort.'

This drew a mild protest from her husband. 'Molly! He's harmless . . . You have to know how to handle him.'

She smiled, not very pleasantly. 'Unlike you, Jerry, I have no wish to handle him.'

'Perhaps you could let me have the names of two or three other guests who might be more specific in their recollections?'

'Must we, sergeant? I hate the idea of my guests being pestered by this sort of thing.'

Kersey and Dixon left with three names, grudgingly given.

'Willy Goppel must have been quite a character. He had a substantial stake in property – Crowther estimates it as something over four-hundred thousand at present values – but he seems to have had a thing about not letting his right hand know what his left was doing. He spread his work around. Crowther drew up leases and dealt with the legal side generally; Cassells and White collected rents, prepared inventories and found tenants for his properties while Fiske's outfit dealt with his accounts, insurance, investment and tax.'

Wycliffe and Scales were treating themselves to a decent meal in the restaurant opposite Paul's Court which was run by a very fat woman of benevolent aspect. She seemed to have a regular clientele for the atmosphere was chummy and from time to time a little man in a chef's hat put his head through the serving hatch to exchange pleasantries with particular customers. There was not much choice of either food or wine but what there was was good. A diminutive waitress of uncertain age answered to the name of Pearl. She served the tables with assistance from the proprietress when it was needed, but mostly the fat woman presided impressively at the bar and indicated what was to be done by restrained gestures of a plump, many-ringed hand. From time to time she shifted herself to make a royal progress round the tables with an apt word at each.

'Freddie will be a wealthy young man. According to Crowther he gets everything except for a few legacies of four thousand each to the Ward children, Yvette, and the landlord at Bickersleigh.'

The little waitress presented them with the cheese board and they helped themselves.

'No pointers?'

Scales shook his head. 'Nothing very obvious. Bishop has made himself a bit of a pain in the neck to Crowther and the estate agents but they don't take him very seriously. What is odd, neither of them have any idea why Goppel wanted him out.'

Wycliffe told him about the Toyland project.

Scales perched a knob of Stilton on a tiny water biscuit and popped it into his mouth. 'I suppose it takes all sorts but if Freddie knew about this it could be a pointer to him and his pal. But there's another oddity.' He took from his wallet the list of local firms which Wycliffe had seen in Willy's desk.

'I saw that and it didn't mean much to me.'

'Nor to me, but I rang round a few of the firms listed and now I'm not so sure.'

'Could you manage a brandy?'

'Why not? But what are we celebrating?'

Wycliffe grinned. 'Stalemate. But what about that list?'

'Yes, well, I rang City Butchers first and the chap who

runs it told me that Willy had rung him a couple of months back with some yarn about looking for additional insurance cover and could he recommend anybody. The bloke said he did all his insurance through a broker. Willy asked which companies issued the policies and he was told that the business was spread around – vehicles, buildings, employers' and public liability and so on. Willy said that he was only interested in buildings and he was then told that the firm's buildings were insured with the Eagle.'

'So? Sounds straightforward. Willy seems to have been a cautious chap.'

'Yes, but he got nothing useful, it was all too vague – no mention of rates, type of cover – anything anybody would want to know. And it was the same with the other firms on the list I contacted. Not a word about anything useful. In any case that's what brokers are for – to get the best deal for a client.'

Wycliffe shrugged. 'You think there's something in it, John?'

'If there is, I'm damned if I can see what; but it's odd. After all, Willy couldn't have been a novice at this sort of thing.'

They finished their meal and left the restaurant feeling mildy guilty, mildly elated. Outside in Falcon Street it was dusk and street lamps competed with the fading daylight; the air was mild and only a faint breeze disturbed the trees in the churchyard.

Mr Hedley, returning from the verandah to the LSO fortissimo, heard the telephone ringing in the hall. After closing the door into the living-room he answered it but it was some time before he established that it was an incoherent Freddie Goppel at the other end. He understood that Toby was involved with the police.

'For God's sake calm down, Freddie. Has he been

arrested?' Mr Hedley was by no means as senile as his wife pretended.

'I don't know. They say they want him to be examined by a doctor and have a blood test—'

'But why? What's he supposed to have done?'

'They seem to think he . . . that he did the murders.'

'Oh, God!' Mr Hedley gave himself a moment. 'Did they accuse him or say anything definite?'

'I don't think so but—'

'Where are you speaking from?'

'The phone box outside the market?'

Mr Hedley's piping, rather plaintive voice became unusually authoritative. 'Right! Now listen, Freddie. Go back to the flat and when Toby comes home tell him to ring. Say to him that if he doesn't his aunt will be frantic . . .'

'But what if he doesn't come back?'

'If he isn't back by eleven you ring again. Got that?'

'Yes, I think so.'

'Good!'

Mrs Hedley was dozing in her chair. Mr Hedley turned off the radio and she opened her eyes. 'What's the matter? Why did you shut it off? I was listening.'

Wycliffe drove home. Helen was in the living-room with the windows open to the night. He kissed her. Her skin was smooth and glowing and he knew that she had been working in the garden until driven indoors by the darkness.

'Have you had a meal?'

'Scales and I pushed the boat out at a place in Falcon Street.'

'Good for you!'

The little crevasse which divided their days had been safely bridged once more.

In bed Wycliffe dozed fitfully, his mind cluttered with

175

the ill-assorted lumber of the day: pictures, fragments of conversation, vague stirrings of the mind which might have crystallized into ideas. It was characteristic of him that his recollections of people were most vivid; sharp as the focused image of a well-made slide. But they were of no use, portraits in a gallery, instant people without past or future; Lennon, Bishop, Natalie, the Fiskes, the Wards, the Hedleys and the gynandrous Freddie. Wycliffe was on the threshold of deeper sleep when he remembered the little slip of paper on which Willy had listed several local firms and their insurers. Scales had said: 'that is what brokers are for, to get the best possible deal for a client . . . After all, Willy was no novice at this kind of thing.'

But Fiske was a broker and Willy's accountant. If Willy wanted advice all he had to do was cross the Court! In his dreamy state this, for some reason, struck him as amusing and he went to sleep smiling.

CHAPTER NINE

According to the police surgeon Lennon's body was whole and without blemish, Kersey's search had discovered nothing incriminating in his flat, but against this Kersey was satisfied that as an alibi the Grenville Road party was a dead duck.

'There's no doubt he arrived there between half-past nine and ten or that he left round three but what he or any of them did in the meantime, God alone knows. It was one of those come-and-go-as-you-please affairs and upwards of fifty people did. Buffet food, help-yourself drinks and the odd spot of fornication upstairs. The thing spread over the whole house and garden. What's more, the Hobson house is only six minutes walk from here if you follow the pedestrian paths, and no more than four on a bike.'

'So,' said Wycliffe, 'Lennon is still a candidate.'

Scales, Kersey and Wycliffe were having their morning conference in the largest of the compartments in the police van.

Scales said, 'If he used his bike to get to and from the Court he would have been fairly conspicuous late at night, it might be worth checking with the lads on the cars.'

Kersey scowled. 'Sitting on their backsides in their cars they see damn all. If Lennon used the paths, only an old-fashioned beat bobby would have had a chance of seeing him.' He stopped and glanced at Wycliffe to see if he had put both feet where angels feared to tread. Cars versus foot-patrols was still a live issue in the force. But Wycliffe was grinning.

'There's no harm in asking the car patrols and, luckily, there are still a few ordinary foot-slogging folk about so why not a house-to-house in the immediate neighbourhood?'

Scales nodded. 'I'll see to it.'

'And John – what about the insurance angle? I think it's worth following up.'

Scales agreed. 'I'm going to visit each of the firms on Willy's list; it's easier to talk man-to-man. After that we can make up our minds whether there's anything in it or not.' He stood up. 'I'll be getting a move on.'

Shortly after Scales had left a constable came in with a package. 'Just delivered from forensic, sir.'

It was Yvette's watch. The brief report which accompanied it was about as informative as one could reasonably expect. Wycliffe read it aloud: ' "The fibres entangled in the bracelet were woollen, of two colours, probably spun together. In which case the garment from which they came would be of a golden-brown colour, it was probably machine knitted, and of good quality. Such wool is commonly made up into jumpers, cardigans, sweaters, etcetera and these are widely sold in the better chain-stores." '

Kersey was unimpressed. 'When we find him we can ask him if he's got a golden-brown etcetera.'

Wycliffe went on: 'There's more. "A link in the bracelet is damaged, leaving a curved fragment of sharply pointed metal almost like a hook. This might easily have caught in a woollen garment of the kind described and, in a laboratory test, the watch, caught in this way, remained attached for fifteen minutes during which time the wearer of the garment was going about his usual laboratory duties." '

'So the guy has a golden-brown pullover or cardigan. I've got one myself.'

The little watch lay on the table between them and for some reason the sight of it stirred Wycliffe to quite unprofessional bitterness and anger.

Mrs Hedley glanced up at the clock. 'It's time you were going, it seems they're there by half-past eight. You must insist on seeing the superintendent.'

'They're bound to ask me why I didn't tell them before. What do I say? That I forgot?'

His wife was contemptuous. 'If you do you might as well not go. Tell them you didn't realize how important it was until you'd talked it over with me.'

When he reached the police van the door was shut and he knocked timidly. A young man opened the door. 'Yes, sir? What can we do for you?'

Hedley told him who he was. 'I would like a word with the superintendent.'

'Mr Hedley from the Court?'

'Yes.'

'Come in.'

Hedley found himself in a little cubicle with a bench seat and a table at which the young man had been working.

'Take a pew, I'll see if the super is free.'

After a very short wait he was taken to a larger room where the superintendent was seated with Sergeant Kersey who recognized him and greeted him in a friendly way.

Mr Hedley found it surprisingly easy to tell his story.

'You say you saw Bishop from your verandah. What time was this?'

'About half-past eleven, I can't say to a few minutes.'

'He was coming out of Goppel's yard?'

179

Mr Hedley hesitated. 'I'm almost sure he was, but it's just possible he had come through the iron gate from Church Lane.'

The superintendant said, 'It's quite a way from your verandah to Goppel's yard . . .'

'Too far for an old man to see in the dark,' Hedley chuckled. 'You're right there. But there's a light just by the little gate and I could see clearly that it was a man though at that distance I didn't know that it was Bishop.'

'What made you notice the man in particular?'

Hedley considered. 'Well, he was behaving oddly, sort of stealthy, then he ran a few steps until he was hidden from me by the tree. When he came out on the other side of the tree he was walking normally though a bit unsteady, and as he got to his own house I saw that it was Bishop. He let himself in with a key.'

'You are willing to make a statement to that effect, Mr Hedley?'

'Oh, yes; that's what I've come for.'

Hedley looked from one to the other of them, wondering what was coming next. It was Kersey, who said, 'You used to work for the council, Mr Hedley, I believe?'

'Yes. I worked there for forty-three years and finished up as deputy head clerk in the Treasurer's department. Then they started to computerize everything and I was too old to start learning all the new tricks so I took the offer of early retirement.'

'And later you worked in Mr Fiske's office?'

'I did. Four years full-time, three years part-time – three days a week. I packed that in last year.'

Wycliffe said, 'Were you his head clerk?'

The old man shook his head. 'Oh, no, that was Jim Staples – he's still there but I hear that he's retiring shortly.' He chuckled, 'Martin Fiske is clever; he employs oldish men who, for one reason or another,

180

have accepted early retirement, then he doesn't pay them the professional rate for the job. All the same, I don't complain, the money came in handy.'

'Didn't Mr Fiske do Willy Goppel's accounts?'

'Oh, yes. Willy was one of Fiske's clients.'

'I believe the firm dealt with all the administration of the concerns they looked after.'

'Oh, yes, everything. "We do your paper-work" was the motto. Accounting, income tax, V.A.T., insurance, everything – even invoicing and merchants' ledger accounts in some cases.'

'Did you deal with insurance?'

'Not me, personally. Mr Fiske dealt with insurance and investment himself. He was an investment and insurance broker before he had the bright idea of setting up as a wet nurse to the small business man.'

When Hedley had gone Kersey said, 'That was interesting.'

'Very.'

'Bishop is no fool though he puts on an act. While I can't see him murdering the girl for sex I wouldn't put it beyond him to do her in if she happened along when he was dealing with Goppel. I think we should talk to him, sir.'

'So do I.'

Kersey drove the superintendent to Fenton Street. Wycliffe was silent for most of the way, then he said, 'We've been trying to find people who were about at the time we believe Yvette and Goppel to have been murdered but what about the Ward boy? Did you ask him if he saw anybody? If Yvette left him on that seat in Lodge Road I don't suppose he stayed there all night.'

Henry Ward was beginning to look like Kersey's private incubus. 'I'll catch him during the school lunch-break, sir.'

There were no parking spaces in Fenton Street and

Kersey had to chance his arm amongst the hardware on Bishop's forecourt.

Bishop's receptionist, secretary and general factotum – all eye shadow and blonde ringlets – said she would see if Bishop was free but they followed her into the inner office where he was making entries in a dog-eared notebook. Kersey turned to the girl, 'Don't worry, Miss, we're all in the family.'

Bishop said, 'Feel free. I'm having a busy morning, Freddie Goppel and his keeper have just left.'

'What did they want?'

Bishop lit a cigarette. 'I don't know that it's any of your business, Mr Kersey, but there's no secret about it – not on my side. Freddie has had glad tidings from his papa's solicitor and he's anxious to get his hands on some cash so he's offered to sell me the freehold of this place when the will is proved, in return for some hard cash now. Apparently the lawyer is sticky about making any advance until you people have tidied things up.'

'So your worries about the lease are over?'

Bishop raised his eyebrows. 'So you know about that. Well, I don't say my worries are over exactly, it depends on the price, but I expect we shall work something out.'

Kersey said, 'It's an ill wind.'

'What's that supposed to mean?'

'Did Goppel tell you why he wanted your place?'

'No, but Freddie did.' Bishop chuckled. 'Willy must have been going ga-ga; he wanted to turn this place into a sort of amusement palace for kids. According to Freddie he was willing to put all his money into it. Allowing for proper filial affection and all that crap Freddie must feel a bit relieved that papa went when he did.'

Wycliffe intervened. 'You remember the evening at La Cass when Lennon was showing off Goppel's service papers?'

Bishop nodded. 'I was there; Pongo was well primed that night.'

'And you saw the papers?'

'I saw something he said belonged to Goppel.'

'You know he lost his wallet and those papers that night?'

'I heard it from Natalie afterwards.'

'But you were with him.'

'Part of the time, yes, but I wasn't watching his bloody wallet. He slung his jacket over the back of his chair and he went off to the toilet at least twice to my knowledge.'

'Did you see him home?'

'Christ, no! He had some black coffee and after that he sobered up a bit. I left him to it.' Bishop jabbed his cigarette into an ashtray.

'What time did you get home on Saturday night?'

'Saturday? I've already told Mr Kersey. I spent the evening in The Sportsman's in Falcon Street and arrived home about half-eleven.'

'Walking?'

'Yes. I've already said that too. What is all this?'

'Did you come into the Court through the archway or through the gate from Church Lane?'

Bishop made an angry movement. 'I'll put all this on bloody tape and you can play it over. I came in through the archway.'

'So you were here in the garage at about four when Yvette called to see you; you drove home, left your car and went out again to the pub – is that right?'

'Yes.'

'Did you drop in to see Willy Goppel on your way home?'

Bishop's brown eyes searched Wycliffe's face for some sign but he encountered only a bland expressionless gaze. 'Why should I drop in on Goppel? We weren't on visiting terms.'

'You might have wanted another word with him on the subject of the lease.'

'At that time of night? Anyway, I didn't.'

'Think carefully, Mr Bishop. It's only fair to tell you that you were seen.'

Bishop swivelled round in his chair and glared from Wycliffe to Kersey and back again. 'Are you trying to set me up? Do you think I killed Goppel? Why should I? Do you think I would murder a man over a bloody lease?'

Wycliffe said nothing and Kersey allowed the silence to lengthen uncomfortably before speaking. 'Nobody is trying to set you up but you've got some explaining to do. You were with Lennon at La Cass when he was shooting off his mouth about Goppel's papers, you were with him when he had his wallet nicked, and now we find you paying a late call on Goppel within an hour or so of his death.'

Bishop re-arranged the things on his desk as though playing draughts. 'You bloody coppers have a way of going about your dirty business, I'll say that for you. I'm not sure what sort of a case you could cook up against me but I know I'll bloody soon find out unless I string along. That's the size of it, isn't it?'

'Nobody's threatening you, Bishop.'

Bishop laughed without humour. 'Isn't that what the actress said? All right, I'll tell you what you want to know and I hope to God you'll believe me. It was about half-eleven, as you say. I'd just come through the archway into the Court when I heard a sort of shriek come from Goppel's place. It was cut off short. I'd had quite a lot to drink and I wasn't too sure of myself. I couldn't think what the hell it could be but it certainly sounded as though somebody had hurt themselves bad. Although I was half cut I thought I'd better take a look so I went to Goppel's back door and knocked but there was no answer. I tried the door and it was unlocked so I went in. There was no light in the workshop but there was a light on the stairs so that I could see well enough. The bloody animals were scuffling about like crazy, squeaking and whistling. I shouted, "Are you all right, Goppel?" There was no answer so I shouted again. I thought he might have electrocuted himself or something. I went through the workshop to the bottom of the stairs and I was just going to call again when I saw him. He was hanging from the banisters at the top of the stairs. I reckon it sobered me up a bit. Anyway, it looked as though he'd put his head in the noose on the top landing and just dropped over the banisters. I thought he must have let out that screech as he fell.'

Wycliffe said, 'Was he tied up – bound in any way?'

Bishop shook his head. 'I don't think so except for the rope round his neck.'

'What did you do?'

'Well, first I thought he might not be dead so I went upstairs so that I could see better. He was dead all right; his face looked ghastly.' Bishop lit another cigarette. 'I know I should have called out the bloody marines or something but when you've had as much to do with the fuzz as I have you learn to keep what they call a low profile. Anyway, I was still pretty drunk. There was nothing I could do for the poor bastard and he was sure to be found sooner or later so I just took off for home, a stiff whisky and bed.'

'I suppose you realize now that Goppel must have been dead for some time when you say you found him?'

Bishop nodded. 'Yes, but I didn't think so then.'

'So have you thought any more about that shriek?'

'Of course I've bloody well thought about it and it doesn't make me feel any better to think that it must've been Yvette, poor little sod. The bastard must've been there while I was snooping about and the pity is I didn't snoop a bit more.' He turned to Wycliffe. 'I suppose all this puts me on your little list?'

'Don't worry, Mr Bishop, you were there already. It might help though, in the business of elimination, if you would agree to a simple medical inspection.'

'What for?'

'It seems likely that Yvette struggled with her attacker and she may have scratched him. We would like to make sure that you have no recent unaccounted-for scratches.'

Bishop shrugged. 'Okay.'

'We would also like to borrow the clothing you were wearing on Saturday night. It would help if you would go back to the house with Mr Kersey now and he will collect it.'

'But I've admitted walking through that bloody work-shop.'

'I know, and that will be taken into account.'

Bishop glanced at his watch. 'I've got a customer in twenty minutes. How about if I arrange to meet Mr Kersey at the house in an hour?'

'Very well.'

Kersey stood up and opened the door abruptly to be confronted with the blonde receptionist. 'The draught through that keyhole has blown your eyelashes off, love; you look positively naked.'

'Cheeky pig!'

Back in the car, Kersey said, 'So Freddie, and therefore Lennon, knew all about Willy's scheme for a kids' amusement place.'

'It looks like it.' Wycliffe was not in a talkative mood.

I can think of less compelling motives for murder than half-a-million.'

'I suppose so.'

'It keeps Lennon very much in the picture.'

'Yes.' Wycliffe sat back in the passenger seat and lit his pipe. 'Bishop or Lennon, we haven't enough evidence against either of them to bring a charge, let alone secure a committal.'

Traffic in the city centre was at its peak and they were held up in queues at lights which changed from red to green and back again.

'Bishop, if he was telling the truth, heard Yvette cry out. He must have arrived at the very instant of the killer's encounter with her. According to him Goppel's body was not strapped up so the bonds must have been removed before Yvette came on the scene.'

Kersey let in the clutch and the car shot across an intersection to join the end of another slow-moving snake on the other side. 'So?'

'I'm just trying to visualize what happened.' At the next set of lights he added, 'What puzzles me is how the killer managed to get Goppel tied up without a struggle.'

'Goppel was ill.'

'But he couldn't have counted on that.'

'Housebreakers sometimes truss up the occupant.'

'Yes, but when they do, they're usually armed.'

Kersey nodded. 'That's a point worth bearing in mind.'

When the school broke for lunch at half-past twelve Kersey was outside in his car. He asked a lad who looked like a sixth-former if he knew Henry Ward; the lad said that he did and volunteered to fetch him. A few minutes later Henry arrived.

'What do you want?' Henry was a trifle wary and sullen.

'Hop in, I won't keep you long; something I forgot to ask. When Yvette left you on the seat in Lodge Road, did you start for home at once?'

'Within a couple of minutes.'

'Did you catch a bus?'

187

'I just missed one – very likely the one Yvette caught. I thought it was probably the last for the night so I walked.'

'Once you got to Falcon Street, did you see anyone you knew?'

Henry thought. 'I don't think I saw anybody at all after the square.'

'Any idea what time you got home?'

'I switched on the radio and they were giving the midnight news summary.'

'Did you go straight to bed?'

'Yes.'

'And you are quite sure that you saw nobody in the neighbourhood of Falcon Street?'

'Quite sure.'

'Pity!' Kersey switched on the ignition. 'You'd better go and get your lunch or you won't grow.'

The boy had his hand on the door catch. 'I've just remembered that while I was undressing I happened to look out of the window and I saw Mr Fiske coming home.'

'You mean you saw him drive into the Court?'

'No, he was walking.'

Kersey felt a slight prickling sensation at the back of his neck. 'What time was this?'

'It couldn't have been long after twelve.'

'How was he dressed?'

'I didn't notice – something dark, I think, a mac or coat.'

'Carrying anything?'

Henry giggled. 'Oh yes, he had his briefcase.'

'And that's funny?'

'Oh, it's just a joke in the Court. He has a lady out at Parkeston – somebody from his office – and when he's been there he arrives back late at night, carrying his briefcase and people say, "Fiske working late again," ' He added after a moment, 'Not very funny really.'

188

'But he couldn't have walked from Parkeston, surely?'

'No, I expect he came by taxi. His car was in dock, somebody backed into him.'

'Did you hear a taxi?'

'No, but I wouldn't have noticed.' He hesitated, still with his hand on the door catch. 'What is all this? What's Fiske done?'

'Nothing – nothing at all. I just wondered if he might have seen anything.'

The telephone rang. Joan Fiske was in the kitchen and she went through to the living-room to answer it.

'This is Martin, I shall be home to lunch. I have to pick up some papers for a client.'

She had no opportunity to reply before he replaced the receiver, but she was used to that. She glanced at the clock, it was a quarter to eleven and he would expect his lunch at one. She and Marty would have made do with fish fingers but he would expect something more than that; she busied herself with calculations – what there was in the freezer, how long it would take to thaw and then cook. In the end she decided on cod fillets with white sauce, steamed carrots and boiled potatoes. They would start with tomato juice and finish with ice-cream.

He arrived promptly at one, ate his meal and even complimented her on it. 'I enjoyed that, the sauce was good.' Then he went upstairs. She heard him in the bathroom and when he came down half-an-hour later he had changed into a light-weight suit which he rarely wore and he carried the inevitable briefcase. He paused in the doorway of the living-room, looking back as though he might have forgotten something.

'Oh, I shall be late home, don't wait up for me.'

There was nothing new in all this, it had happened so often as to become almost a ritual but emotionally she had been on a knife edge since before Yvette's funeral and she had all but made an exhibition of herself in front of the superintendent. Seeing her husband, smug and immaculate, casually informing her of his intention at the very last moment, was too much:

'Don't think you're fooling me, you're going to spend half the night with that slut!' She spoke with such intensity and hatred that her voice was barely recognizable.

Fiske looked at her in utter amazement, then his face closed, losing all expression. 'I have no idea what you are talking about.'

'No? Do you think I haven't known all along about that woman? About the flat in Parkeston? Do you think I don't know why I've got to watch every penny, go short myself or keep Marty short? All so that you can play your dirty games with a little whore who is too selfish to take on a man of her own.'

Fiske came back into the room and closed the door. 'You are out of your mind!'

She was scared of him but she had gone too far to draw back. She laughed hysterically. 'Out of my mind, am I? It would be no wonder with you making me a laughing stock of the neighbourhood and everybody gossiping behind my back. But I wouldn't mind all that if you treated me with a bit of consideration in the home, but all I am is a servant; in fact no servant would stand for being treated as you treat me.'

Her voice was letting her down and soon her hysterical anger would dissolve into a flood of tears but she felt an overwhelming desperate need to empty herself of bitterness which she had secreted like venom over months and years. She sat on the nearest chair because she no longer had the strength to stand. 'With these terrible things that have happened in the Court you go off and leave me alone with a helpless, weak-minded boy when we could both be murdered in our beds.

There is a murderer in the Court . . . ' She broke off and looked at him in hatred. 'Sometimes I wonder—'

He had been standing over her, pale but impassive, now – suddenly, his expression changed, he stooped and gripped her by the wrist so that she let out a cry of pain. 'What do you wonder?' His face was close to hers and he forced her to look into his eyes. 'What do you wonder in that twisted little mind of yours? Tell me, I want to know . . . '

She was going to say that she wondered whether he was deliberately trying to drive her into an asylum but now the words would not come, instead she began to sob convulsively and then tears overwhelmed her. He released her arm and stood back, looking down at her. After a little while he went to the door, let himself out and closed it behind him.

In the Court Marty was bouncing a ball on the cobbles. He looked sideways at his father as though half expecting some rebuke but his father strode across to the garages without appearing to notice him.

Wycliffe and Kersey were closeted in the incident-van. It was two-thirty in the afternoon; Thursday – early closing day, all the shops were shut and Falcon Street was deserted. Even the post office was closed. In the church-yard three of four old men shuffled along the gravelled paths, stopping now and then in a patch of sunshine. In the vicarage garden the vicar's little daughter was using her swing. Eek-wok, eek-wok . . .

'I wish to God he'd oil that bloody thing,' Kersey said.

'He probably wouldn't have had a taxi pick him up at the flat.' Wycliffe spoke of Fiske, not the vicar.

Kersey agreed. 'No, I thought of that. I told Dixon and Fowler to enquire about any fares put down in Falcon Street after midnight but I doubt if there will be any.'

The telephone rang. 'Wycliffe.'

It was Scales. 'I won't say too much over the telephone but I think we are on the right track. All the firms on Willy's list with a tick beside them were looked after by Fiske and all of them had been approached by Willy about their insurance position. Two of them have the beginnings of a suspicion what it's all about but I put them off ... Now, sir, it amounts to this, all the insurance firms concerned have regional offices in the city. If I start raising queries with them it might be difficult to keep our inquiry under cover. On the other hand ...'

'Carry on, John, just be as discreet as you can.'

Kersey said, 'What about me, sir?'

'You stay here and hold the fort, I think I'll have a word with Natalie.'

Wycliffe strolled down Falcon Street, past the Dolls' House shop which was already acquiring an air of neglect. He turned in at the archway and crossed the Court to Natalie's. The house had a deserted look but after ringing the bell a couple of times he heard somebody stirring and Natalie came to the door. She was wearing a housecoat, her eyes looked puffy with sleep and it was obvious that she had just run a comb through her hair before answering the door.

'I was lying down, you'd better come in.'

He was taken into the white living-room and swallowed up by one of the armchairs.

'Drink?'

'No, thanks.'

'I need something.' She poured a generous helping of gin into a glass and dashed it with lime. She was pale and there were dark rings under her eyes.

'Are you come to tell me or ask me?'

'To ask. That evening when Lennon was drunk and started showing Goppel's papers around – who was there?'

She stroked her cheek with the lip of her glass but she made no attempt to deny the incident. 'It's some time ago. It was early evening, before anybody much turns up, and we were round the bar. I know Freddie wasn't there. Of course there was Stefan, the barman, me, the girl who plays the accordion – you remember her.'

'Bishop?'

'Yes, Geoff was there, drinking with Pongo . . . and Martin Fiske.'

'With his girl-friend?'

'No, he was alone. I remember him particularly because I was watching him while Pongo was telling his ghastly yarns about what the Nazis did to Jewish girls in concentration camps. I'm sure Pongo makes those yarns up, he's the sort of queer who has it in for women and he broods on that sort of thing. Fiske was lapping it all up, that man gives me the creeps.'

'What about afterwards? You put Lennon at the back and sent Bishop to keep an eye on him . . .'

She gave him a quick look. 'My! You have been doing your homework.'

'Did you notice who went to that table?'

'You mean, who could have nicked Pongo's wallet. I doubt if anybody did. If Pongo can't draw attention to himself one way he will another.'

'You haven't answered my question.'

She sipped her gin. 'I don't know that I can, I had something better to do than nurse Pongo, but the regulars circulate quite a bit. When I happened to be at the end of the room there were four of them at the table – Freddie had turned up and Fiske was with them. Geoff told me afterwards that he was after more of Pongo's fantasies to help him through his nights.'

She swallowed a mouthful of gin and coughed over it. 'Men!'

CHAPTER TEN

Joan Fiske pushed back the debris of her meal, rested her arms on the dining table, placed her head on her arms, and wept. She wept until her anger had drained away, giving place to self-pity, and her hatred had withered, leaving only emptiness. She found that she could look back on what had happened as though two other people had been involved. Wearily she got up from the table, swept back her hair from her eyes, and looked out of the window. Marty was throwing his ball up into the branches of the tree, over and over again. She went slowly upstairs to the bathroom and bathed her face and eyes in cold water. For a time her mind was almost blank, then she began to recall odd phrases of the tirade she had launched against her husband and they repeated themselves in her mind again and again. But they seemed meaningless, she could not associate them with any intense emotion. What was it all about? Why did it happen like this after months – after years?

She went into her bedroom and sat at the dressing-table, brushing her hair with feeble strokes. What would happen when he came home? Would things go on just as before? Did she want them to?

'Oh, God, I don't know!'

'Forget about your husband and concentrate on yourself ... You lack confidence ... especially in yourself ... you have a great deal of moral courage; you are willing to suffer for what you believe to be right and you have the strength to win through ... ' The Tarot. Mrs

Hedley had done her best in difficult circumstances. 'Forget about your husband . . .'

The numbness was wearing off; emotion returned like blood to a chilled limb, bringing pain.

After a while she went downstairs and resumed her normal routine. She cleared away the remains of lunch, washed the dishes and put them away. No evening meal to prepare; she and Marty would have something out of a tin. As she worked, isolated instants of the confrontation presented themselves uninvited to her mind with the clarity of images on a television screen.

'I have no idea what you are talking about.' Amazement, suddenly masked by utter blankness. She could see him plainly, standing in the doorway, half turned towards her. Then he had closed the door and come back into the room. 'You are out of your mind!' More than a figure of speech, for he had always let it be known that Marty's condition arose directly from a history of mental disorder on her side of the family.

He had come to stand over her and she had been scared. She marvelled that she had found the courage and strength to go on. He had towered over her, monumental; and she had known that his expression would be utterly without warmth, lacking even the heat of anger. There was nothing – *nothing* that she could say or do to reach him.

And yet, a moment later, she had looked up into his face, 'Sometimes I wonder—' she had said. That was all. He had gripped her arm painfully, his expression of aloof detachment gone, and in its place – cruelty? No, not cruelty; she had seen his features moulded by cruelty more than once and this was different. Not anger, not hatred, not even contempt – but *fear*.

His face close to hers, forcing her to look into his eyes, 'What do you wonder in that twisted little mind? I want to know.'

But why should he be afraid? It was not possible.

Joan Fiske was not a particularly intelligent woman but she was tenacious, often tediously so, and now she set herself to recall, instant by instant, what exactly had happened before that astounding transformation. She had been speaking of him leaving her alone in the house with only Marty – 'a helpless, weak-minded boy' she had called him, with a sense of betrayal ' . . . we could both be murdered in our beds. *There is a murderer in the Court* . . . ' and then, '*Sometimes I wonder*—'

It was as though she had had a revelation.

'Dear God help me!'

Alison Ward arrived home from school to an empty house. It was Thursday, half-day closing, and Mr and Mrs Ward were visiting relatives in Kingsmeade on the outskirts of the city. Henry was playing cricket in a house match. Alison went to her room and changed her school clothes for jeans and a shirt. It reminded her of Yvette and of Willy Goppel and she felt the tears smarting in her eyes. She was not supposed to be in the house alone – not according to her mother. She had intended to play tennis, then she and Henry would have come home together, but something had gone wrong with the fixtures and the match had been cancelled.

She went down to the living-room with a book and sat on the window-seat with her feet up, reading.

Somebody was ringing the back-door bell, leaning on it apparently, for it never stopped. Perhaps Henry had forgotten his key, but it was too early for Henry. She went downstairs, just a little uneasy, but ashamed of her misgivings. She opened the door to find Mrs Fiske, wildly excited, with Marty behind her.

'I must come in, Alison! You *must* let me in . . .'

'Yes, of course, Mrs Fiske. Come on, Marty . . .' Marty was hanging back.

'Lock the door, Alison – lock it, for God's sake!'

Mrs Fiske was breathing hard and the stairs taxed her but there was nowhere else Alison could take them. She led the way into the living-room, wondering what on earth was wrong and feeling helpless. Mrs Fiske collapsed on the settee.

'Ask your mother—'

'But mother and father are out, Mrs Fiske, they've gone over to Kingsmeade. Is there anything I can do? Would you like a cup of tea?'

Mrs Fiske had her hand to her bosom and her breathing, which had been painfully audible, was subsiding. 'It's my husband . . .'

'Mr Fiske – is he hurt or something?'

She lowered her voice to a dramatic whisper. 'Hurt? He's a murderer!'

'But—'

'I know! He murdered Willy Goppel and he murdered little Yvette.'

Alison, bewildered and frightened as she was, could not help wondering at the blend of horror and triumph with which the frantic woman made her pronouncement. But it seemed to calm her and Alison saw for the first time that she was clutching a much folded piece of newspaper.

'I don't know how I was so blind! He didn't come home until after midnight and he didn't have his car – he only got it back yesterday . . .'

Her words came in short bursts with intervals during which she strove to control her emotion. Marty stood by the window, looking at the floor.

'He wasn't even wearing one of his good suits and I should have known he'd never have gone to her like that – never in a million years.'

Alison perched on the edge of one of the dining chairs, utterly at a loss. Mrs Fiske got up and moved over to the window where she peered down into the Court.

'I would have gone to the Hedleys but he knows I sometimes go there and he might . . . Then I thought if I came here, there would be your brother and your father . . .

'A few days before I had to take Marty to Bristol for his treatment and while I was away he *turned out the box-room!*'

'The box-room?' Alison was mystified.

Mrs Fiske turned from the window. 'Yes. You think I'm mad, Alison, but I'm not. He's never done a hand's turn in the house since I married him and then, suddenly . . . "I've thrown out a lot of old rubbish," he said.'

She moved uncertainly to the table where she unfolded her crumpled piece of newspaper and spread it flat, smoothing it with her long thin hands. 'Look at that – it's from yesterday's paper. See what it says under the picture: "A webbing belt as used by the armed services. The police believe that service webbing, easily obtained from government-surplus stores, was used to bind the murdered man."'

She looked at Alison with great intensity and said, slowly, 'His father was in the regular army and he came to live with us before he died. He had a cupboard full of stuff like that.' After a moment she added with a bitter smile, 'He didn't have to go to any store.'

Alison wished that her parents would come – Henry, anybody . . . Marty shuffled his feet and looked at his mother with pleading eyes. 'Home? Go home?'

Martin Fiske sat at his desk with a client's file open in front of him but he could not concentrate. That lunch-time scene had taken him completely by surprise and at one point he had reacted spontaneously, without proper thought, indeed with no thought at all. A lesson for the future.

Odd, why her melodramatic outburst upset me.

I've taken everything in my stride, even when they found out that Goppel had been murdered . . . *Murder* – so much nonsense talked about murder . . . One is brainwashed into believing that murder is a tremendous act, leaving its mark – the Mark of Cain. Mystical nonsense! But it worried me . . . How would I feel afterwards? What would it be like to have killed a man? Would it be possible to behave normally? Would I feel remorse?

If I had known that I would have to deal with the girl as well I should have drawn back . . . With Goppel I felt nothing – nothing at all. I did what I had planned with as little emotion as I would play a round of golf . . . Finding the old fool asleep made it easier . . .

The girl was different . . . sex . . . her struggles excited me and I was tempted. But for that blundering oaf, Bishop . . . Afterwards I felt as though I really had screwed the little slut . . . I kept her shirt . . . Stupid!

I was obsessed by getting her out of the house – a mistake. Left where she was she would have been down to Goppel . . . They wouldn't have looked any further then . . .

Remorse? A fiction. Killing is making a hole in water . . . That silly, shabby little shop will disappear from the street and there is one sexy young tramp the less . . .

Against that, I am safe.

There are those who hesitate and those who act. Goppel was a fool but he spotted the tip of the iceberg – a few piddling insurance policies allowed to lapse for a time before being renewed with another company.

'I'll give you time to get straightened out, Fiske . . . '

Patronising bastard! No notion of the kind of man he was dealing with.

'Penny for them.' Fiona, standing in the doorway, smiling.

'Sorry, I was day-dreaming.'

'Obviously. The superintendent is back with a sergeant and they want a word.'

'Give me a minute, then show them in.'

The thing is to be on one's guard but to behave normally. A mouthful of brandy . . .

'Ah, do sit down, Superintendent. I'm afraid you've caught me at a bad time, I have an appointment in five minutes.'

The superintendent in the client's chair, he's left his sergeant outside.

'One or two questions, Mr Fiske.'

His manner is different. No apology for calling without an appointment. Not the slightest sign of friendliness . . . Disturbing.

'What questions?' Mistake number one. Better to keep quiet. Look of bored attention.

'Can you remember when you arrived home on Saturday night.'

'Saturday?'

'The night Goppel and Yvette were killed.'

Careful! 'I think I told you that I did not go out on Saturday night.'

'What you said was, that you were not out late.'

'Well?' When in doubt, play for time.

'You were seen in the Court at about midnight.'

A nasty jolt. Of course, it was on the cards; the bloody busy-bodies never sleep.

'A man doesn't want his comings and goings known to everybody.'

'If you are about to say that you spent part of the night at Parkeston, I should tell you that we know your car was out of commission and public transport stops shortly after eleven.'

Think! Keep a clear head. Taxi? Easily checked.

Borrowed car? Ditto . . . Only one possible answer. 'I did not go to Parkeston on Saturday.'

'So what were you doing in the Court at midnight?'

This looks better. An easy laugh. 'I feel such a damn fool! All I was doing was taking a stroll. I couldn't sleep so I got up and dressed and went for a turn round the block.'

'Carrying your briefcase?'

Still not a glimmer of expression; clinically cold. Only way, a flat denial. 'I was certainly not carrying my briefcase.'

The bastard knows how to keep a poker face . . . Where to look? Suddenly it's difficult to know how to hold my head, where to direct my eyes. I'm losing my grip on normal behaviour. My hands are wrong – clasped together on the desk, but too tightly. I can see the whites of my knuckles. Relax! A glance at the clock. 'I hope this isn't going to take too long, Superintendent?' That's better.

'When you went for your stroll, how were you dressed?'

'Dressed?' What the hell is this about? 'Not very elegantly, just a pair of slacks and an old mackintosh.'

'No jacket?'

What in God's name is the man after? 'No jacket, but I really can't see why all this should interest you. In fact, I wore a cardigan.'

'And shirt, pants and socks?'

'Naturally.'

'I would like to see the clothes you wore, Mr Fiske.'

God! I cut her nails. 'Are you making some fantastic accusation against me, Superintendent?'

Still not the slightest change of expression. 'I am asking you to let me see the clothes you wore on Saturday night.'

'And if I refuse?'

'You have that right but, of course, the matter would not end there.'

A threat! Christ! My lips are trembling and it's affecting my speech. Ask for a solicitor? An admission of guilt. Better to carry it a bit further first. Try to find out what they know. 'All right, Superintendent, I've nothing to hide but, I warn you, I do not take this intrusion lightly. After I have seen my next client I will go with you and you can inspect my whole wardrobe if you wish.'

'I'm sorry, Mr Fiske, but it will have to be now.'

God! He must be sure of his ground. 'Very well, if you insist; I will ask my secretary to apologize for me.'

'Good!'

The staff watching me as I go through with a policeman in tow. Fiona in the outer office with the typists and the sergeant. She gives me an odd look. She's as stupid as the rest. I tell her to let Staples deal with old Morse when he comes.

Outside, shiny new Ford parked on yellow lines. Beginning to rain; big spots on the pavement. In the back with Wycliffe, the sergeant driving.

'Nice car. Granada, isn't it?'

'Yes.'

'Always a bit heavy on petrol, these Fords, don't you think?'

No answer.

Oh, God, I feel sick! . . . Five o'clock . . . Five o'clock. What does time matter any more? Meaningless! All the time there is . . . The streets slide by . . . already I feel cut off – apart. Raining hard now, the wind-shield wipers sweeping back and forth . . . Shall I ever drive again? Mustn't lose my nerve . . . I read somewhere that three out of four criminals convict themselves . . . I wonder what prison is really like. Do they make allowances for a man's class? They can't just put you in a cell with . . . Oh Christ!

Turning into the Court now. Like a stranger, seeing it for the first time . . . Puddles in the cobbles. Nobody about but somebody is watching; somebody always is. Two men in my garden, one holding a large umbrella . . .

'What are they doing in my garden? Are they policemen?'

'One is, the other is a scientific officer from the forensic laboratory. They are taking samples of ash from your incinerator.'

'But they have no right!'

'You will have ample chance to protest.'

No sign of Joan or the boy . . . Have they taken them away? The door of the house is wide open and there is a policeman on the verandah. Protest.

'This is beyond everything! Searching my house without giving me the opportunity to be there!'

'The door was found open, sir, there was no one about and none of our chaps have been inside.' The policeman on the verandah defending himself.

'You hear that, Mr Fiske?' Wycliffe's voice, level and cold. 'Perhaps you will lead the way.'

No sign of anybody. 'Joan! Marty!' Where the hell can they be?

Old man Hedley watching from his bloody verandah. Upstairs in my bedroom. The wardrobe. 'Here you are. Superintendent . . . '

Mackintosh, trousers, zip-fronted cardigan, shoes . . . 'That's the best I can do. My underclothes and socks have been laundered and I've no idea which they were.' Sounds reasonable and has the advantage of being true. Each item goes into a separate polythene bag.

'Your clothes will go to the forensic laboratories, Mr Fiske, but they will be returned to you.'

Labelled Courtroom exhibits A, B, C . . . They say sex offenders and child murderers are roughed up in prison. But she was fifteen and I didn't rape her . . .

Kersey comes in. 'The small room at the back, is that your study, Mr Fiske? We are going to search it, I think you should be there.'

My own little room. Wycliffe stands by the window, looking down into the yard; Kersey prying and poking into all my things . . . God, how I HATE them!

My little cupboard, my shelves, my books, my filing cabinet, my desk . . . I am ignored. They do not even look at me!

But they find NOTHING. The bastards are slipped up after all.

'I hope that now, Superintendent, you will realize—'
God! Kersey is pulling out the drawers of the desk . . .

Kersey was removing the desk drawers and when he had done so he reached into the dusty, cob-webbed recesses behind. He came out with a couple of bulky paper-back novels of the kind which bristle with four-letter words, then a liberally illustrated book on punishment through the ages, another on flagellation and a so-called *Study of Sexual Perversion and Deviant Behaviour*.

Wycliffe looked at the little heap. Frailty thy name is man. But if that were all . . .

Then Kersey, like a conjuror at the climax of his act, produced a package wrapped in newspaper and a gun, an old service revolver. The package was soft and yielding. Without looking at Fiske he removed the wrapping and a springy cotton garment, carelessly folded, lay on the desk. He spread it out – a T-shirt with 'Restricted Area' printed in red across the front. No blood.

'If you insist on writing out a statement for yourself, you should start with the declaration required by Judges' Rules, otherwise it won't count for much.'

Kersey and Fiske sat one on each side of a small table in a bare interview room in the Mallet Street police station. A uniformed constable was posted at the door.

'I'll dictate the formula.'

Fiske picked up the 'Bic' supplied by a benevolent state.

Against Wycliffe's advice Fiske had refused to call a solicitor and had insisted on making a statement which he would write himself. He began to write, apparently calm, pausing now and then over the choice of a word.

During his years in the force Kersey had seen many men driven into that last corner, finally convinced that no amount of lying or twisting will save them from the dock. At that point the professional stops talking and waits for his lawyer. Others react according to temperament. The resigned shrug and say, 'You can't win 'em all!', the optimists sing their little heads off to buy goodwill, others simply deflate. Kersey had expected Fiske to deflate but he bounced.

After the scene in his study he seemed to accept trial and conviction as inevitable and, scared as he undoubtedly was, he was even more concerned to establish that what he had done had required courage, imagination and resource. If he had to go to gaol, everyone would know that it was for a crime cleverly conceived and skilfully executed but dogged by ill-luck. He would be in the books.

'He should have saved it for the newspapers,' Kersey said.

At half-past ten Wycliffe was in one of the little

cubicles of the incident-van, reading a photostat of Fiske's statement – all twelve sheets of it. To begin with it was both legible and coherent but as he turned the pages legibility, coherence and even relevance suffered. Which might do Fiske some good. In the hands of a clever counsel and a pliant psychiatrist it could provide the germ of a plea of diminished responsibility. They wouldn't get away with it but it might temper the mood of judge and jury.

Wycliffe growled to himself, 'Not my affair!'

The telephone rang.

'Wycliffe.'

'It's me.' Helen, his wife. 'Is it all over?'

'All over, I shall be home inside the hour.'

He left the van, feeling deflated. Falcon Street was deserted and it was still drizzling rain. Before going to his car he walked the few steps to Paul's Court, through the archway and into the Court. The wet cobbles gleamed in the lamplight. Willy Goppel's house was in darkness; Natalie was at her club. There were lights in the Wards' and the Fiskes'. As he crossed the Court he was aware of a still figure on the Hedleys' verandah and he could hear, faintly, the sound of a piano. He went up the steps to the Fiskes' front door and rang the bell.

He had arranged for a policewoman to keep Mrs Fiske company until she had made other arrangements or felt able to be left on her own. But it was Mrs Fiske who answered the door and he was immediately aware of a new briskness in her manner.

'Oh, Mr Wycliffe! I'm afraid I sent your young woman away. It was kind of you to arrange it but, as I told Mrs Ward, Marty and I will manage very well on our own.'

'You are sure?'

'Oh yes, quite sure, but thank you for coming.' She stood, holding the door only partly open, 'I don't want

206

to be rude but Marty and I are having a late supper – a little treat for him; he's had such an upsetting day. I'm sure you'll understand . . . '

'Of course! I'll say good-night, then.'

'Good-night, Mr Wycliffe, good-night.'

The door closed before he reached the bottom of the steps.

THE END

A SELECTED LIST OF CRIME NOVELS
AVAILABLE FROM CORGI BOOKS

THE PRICES SHOWN BELOW WERE CORRECT AT THE TIME OF GOING TO PRESS.
HOWEVER TRANSWORLD PUBLISHERS RESERVE THE RIGHT TO SHOW NEW RETAIL
PRICES ON COVERS WHICH MAY DIFFER FROM THOSE PREVIOUSLY ADVERTISED IN
THE TEXT OR ELSEWHERE.

☐	14119 4	A Hovering of Vultures	Robert Barnard	£3.99
☐	13361 2	A Little Local Murder	Robert Barnard	£3.99
☐	13932 7	A Fatal Attachment	Robert Barnard	£3.99
☐	13232 2	Wycliffe and the Beales	W.J. Burley	£2.99
☐	14264 6	Wycliffe and the Dead Flautist	W.J. Burley	£3.99
☐	14268 9	Wycliffe and the Tangled Web	W.J. Burley	£3.99
☐	14109 7	Wycliffe and the Cycle of Death	W.J. Burley	£2.99
☐	13689 1	Wycliffe and Death in Stanley Street	W.J. Burley	£2.99
☐	14267 0	Wycliffe and the Four Jacks	W.J. Burley	£3.99
☐	13435 X	Wycliffe and the Quiet Virgin	W.J. Burley	£3.99
☐	14266 2	Wycliffe and the Scapegoat	W.J. Burley	£3.99
☐	12805 8	Wycliffe and the Schoolgirls	W.J. Burley	£3.99
☐	14269 7	Wycliffe's Wild-Goose Chase	W.J. Burley	£3.99
☐	13436 8	Wycliffe and the Winsor Blue	W.J. Burley	£3.99
☐	12804 X	Wycliffe and the Pea-Green Boat	W.J. Burley	£3.99
☐	14265 4	Wycliffe and the Last Rites	W.J. Burley	£3.99
☐	14221 2	Wycliffe and the Dunes Mystery	W.J. Burley	£3.99
☐	14117 8	Wycliffe and How to Kill a Cat	W.J. Burley	£3.99
☐	14115 1	Wycliffe and the Guilt Edged Alibi	W.J. Burley	£3.99
☐	14205 0	Wycliffe and the Three-toed Pussy	W.J. Burley	£3.99
☐	14043 0	Shadowplay	Frances Fyfield	£4.99
☐	14174 7	Perfectly Pure and Good	Frances Fyfield	£4.99
☐	13840 1	Closed Circle	Robert Goddard	£4.99
☐	13839 8	Hand In Glove	Robert Goddard	£4.99
☐	13144 X	Past Caring	Robert Goddard	£4.99
☐	13941 6	Alibi in Time	June Thomson	£3.99
☐	13982 3	A Touch of Frost	R.D. Wingfield	£4.99
☐	13981 5	Frost at Christmas	R.D. Wingfield	£4.99
☐	13985 8	Night Frost	R.D. Wingfield	£4.99